Stephanie Dunk has always believed that she would write a very special book, but the timing has never been right until now.

This is the first of many books based on her belief in the powerful energy that lies under the ground beneath our feet. There have been many books written about fairies, elves, gnomes, witches and wizards, but this book focuses on what is hiding underneath the mushrooms.

This book is an adventure into the fairy world and starts on level one. As you dive deeper into the book, you will discover that there are many levels and many kinds of energy. Some are good and some are bad. Some are positive while others are negative. There are both happy and sad energies hiding down there.

Stephanie Dunk

LEVEL CONTROL

Prepare for a Journey

AUSTIN MACAULEY PUBLISHERS™

LONDON · CAMBRIDGE · NEW YORK · SHARJAH

A CIP catalogue record for this title is available from the British Library.

ISBN 9781528909815 (Paperback)
ISBN 9781528931465 (ePub e-book)

www.austinmacauley.com

First Published (2021)
Austin Macauley Publishers Ltd
25 Canada Square
Canary Wharf
London
E14 5LQ

A big, big thank you:

To my son, James, and my daughter, Chloe, for listening and always being there for me.

To Sharon, a good friend and partner to my son, who helped me with ideas on how to market my book.

For all my family and friends, especially my parents, for their love and support.

For all of my grandchildren – Freddie, Jasmine, Mae and Jake – whom I am very proud of.

For all of my family and friends for investing their money in *Level Control*.

For Dave, who believed in my book from the start and invested some of the money to publish *Level Control*.

To my wonderful friend Julia for all her support in bringing together this book.

To Alice, Rosle and Tilly, the children of the future, who helped me create all of my ideas and inspired me to think like a child.

To the students from Thomas Peacocke Community College, who did the illustrations.

Finally, to my parents, who gave me a wonderful childhood, where I was able to develop my ideas about the three mushrooms.

Table of Contents

Introduction

My name is Stephanie Dunk. I have always believed that I would write a very special book but the timing has never been right, until now. This is my first book of many based on my belief that there is a powerful energy under the ground. Many books have been written about fairies, elves, gnomes, witches and wizards. I feel that there are fairies at the bottom of the garden, but what's more interesting is what is underneath the mushrooms, below the ground.

My story is an adventure into the fairy world which starts on level one. As you read, you will discover that there are many levels underneath the ground and many energies; some good, some bad, some negative, some positive and some sad.

Fairies, elves, gnomes, witches and wizards, as well as other characters, will appear on different levels. The title of my book is *Level Control*. Can you reach each level and stay in control? The journey has begun. Follow me into the unknown and trust that you can be in control as we reach each level together.

Chapter One
The Sad Face

My story begins in a tiny village called Witterlam. The village was named after the many lambs and sheep that graze in nearly every second field. In fact, many of these lambs and sheep could tell you their stories about the special mushrooms where the fairy folk live. The village has one main street and no shops, although the local garage sells many items. Sweets, pies, and milk can all be purchased as well as petrol and plenty of jokes and banter from Mike, the owner. Now, he could tell you a tale or two. The many shops which once stood in the village have now disappeared, leaving the village life even quieter than before.

There is a little school down the lane where Luke and Sophie meet and become the best of friends. Sophie lives in the centre of the village whilst Luke lives around the corner and down the lane. Their friendship has lasted three years, ever since Luke discovered that Sophie was being bullied at school. Luke came to Sophie's rescue and she has not forgotten it. Now, they are both ten and their relationship has become very strong and solid. You could say boyfriend and girlfriend, although, Luke always shies away from this remark. Every morning, five days a week, they both meet by the phone box opposite Sophie's house, at 8:30, Monday to Friday, which gives them plenty of time to talk about the mushrooms at the bottom of Sophie's garden. At night, when Luke and Sophie should be sleeping, they watch the mushrooms growing inch by inch. Strange, because in the morning, they were exactly the same size as the night before. It is extra lucky for Luke because, although, he lives around the corner and down the lane, his garden backs on to Sophie's back garden; so, he can see this too. Each morning, it takes Luke and Sophie ten minutes to measure each mushroom and at night, they see them growing. Why then, in the morning, are they the same size? Magical, they certainly are. It seems that the mushrooms only get bigger by night and when it's a full moon, they double in size. This, of course, is the children's focus in life, to understand the reason why this is happening at the bottom of Sophie's garden.

It was Monday morning 8:30 am and Luke had arrived at Sophie's house and he was greeted at the front door by Sophie's mother, Mrs Barker.

"On time, as usual, Luke, never too late and never too early," remarked Sophie's mother. "Step in, Luke, she won't be long."

"By the way, Sophie," Mrs Barker called out, "have you seen my tape measure?"

Appearing at the bottom of the stairs, looking very sheepishly at her mother, Sophie replied, "It's in the garden shed, Mum."

"What is it doing in there?" asked Mrs Barker. Responding quickly, Sophie replied, "I have been measuring the fish in the garden, they are getting bigger every day."

This made Sophie feel quite good as she knew that the fish were eating too much and they were getting bigger every day. Mrs Barker started to fuss about the tape measure so Sophie and Luke grabbed their coats and their bags, not forgetting their lunchboxes, and said their goodbyes as they turned and closed the door.

"Thank goodness for that, I thought we would have to invest in a new tape measure," said Sophie.

Luke replied, "You don't think that your mum knows about the mushrooms, do you, Sophie?"

"No, of course not, don't be so silly. She hardly goes out in the garden, even the washing line is not used since Dad bought her that second washing machine that dries clothes."

"They call it a tumble dryer," replied Luke, "not a washing machine."

"I don't care what it is called as long as she remembers to dry my new dress in it for Rachel's party next Saturday."

Sophie seemed quite stressed about the drying machine so Luke changed the subject quickly.

"So, what time shall I come around tonight?" asked Luke keenly.

"Better leave it until 5:30, Mum is having a friend over for tea so it will be later than our normal time of 5:00; they talk a lot and laugh too much, it's a wonder I get any tea when she comes around."

Luke and Sophie started their walk through the village, turning right into the school lane. It was not until they had reached their school that they both realised that their regular event before school had been missed; the mushrooms had not been measured. Not a good start to their day, in fact, both of them found it very difficult to concentrate in their class. At last, the day ended and they raced back home together, but on reaching Sophie's house and opening the garden shed door, they realised to their horror that the tape measure was no longer there, which could only mean one thing, Sophie's mum had moved it earlier in the day. Now, what were they going to do?

Luke then came up with a brilliant idea: "How about my ruler?" he said.

"Great idea," said Sophie. "Where is it?"

Luke remembered he had left his ruler in his desk back at school.

"So much for your big ideas," said Sophie with a stern voice.

"So, what big ideas have you got?" replied Luke.

"Well," said Sophie, "no measuring today."

"Okay," replied Luke. "Let's go and have a look anyway." The garden was quite wet as it was the start of spring. Summer was just around the corner, even the grass seemed longer than yesterday, but only a fraction. Passing the fishpond, Luke and Sophie started to run as they were excited to see the mushrooms again. There were three mushrooms yesterday and still three today. The two mushrooms each side of the centre mushroom seemed just like yesterday's, but the centre mushroom was very different. It had doubled in size and had developed three large rings around the top, two of these rings were completely circular but the third was in the shape of a triangle, which seemed very odd. The stalk seemed to be longer than the others and all three mushrooms were very straight and proud. Luke and Sophie knew already however much they tugged and pulled, the mushrooms would stand still, solid in the ground. Nothing seemed to damage them. They seemed to be there for good and in the children's eyes, forever and ever.

"Teatime," shouted a voice from the house. It was Mrs Barker calling from the kitchen window.

"You had better go home and come back after tea," said Sophie.

"Okay," replied Luke. "But don't forget we need the tape measure."

"I won't forget, Luke," replied Sophie as she ran into the kitchen and Luke went out the gate. Tea time seemed to go on forever and ever. Sophie's mum kept talking and laughing, delaying everything, so by the time Luke came back, they were only eating their first course. *No time for pudding,* thought Sophie, as she pushed her food down her throat.

"Guess what've I got for you all?" Mrs Barker said. "Your favourite, Sophie, lemon cheesecake."

She's done this on purpose, Sophie thought to herself. *Perhaps she does know about the magic of the mushrooms. Perhaps this is why she has the tape measure. Perhaps she is measuring them too.* Sophie's imagination was working overtime. As much as Sophie loved lemon cheesecake, now was not the time to indulge. So, she made an excuse and left the table to meet Luke outside in the garden once again.

"So what excuse was it this time?" Luke asked Sophie.

"Toothache," replied Sophie. It was the first thing that came into her head. In fact, she got a lot of toothaches these days.

It was 5:45 pm and just starting to get dark. Sophie's mum was quite happy with the two children going into the garden as long as they did not leave, but she insisted that Sophie come in at six, only 15 minutes for that last check of the day. The three mushrooms were still standing straight and proud. The middle one, the larger of the two, seemed to be a different colour tonight, almost blue, in fact. The children bent down to take a closer look. It was then they noticed a small wing, the size of a butterfly's, on the top of this mushroom. But it did not belong to a butterfly, it belonged to a fairy called Flueller. In her haste on seeing the children, she lost her wing, but fairies could still fly with one wing, even though their journey was a slower one. Luke noticed the wing first; he picked it up gently and placed it in the palm of his hand.

"So, where did this come from?" he asked Sophie.

"How should I know?" replied Sophie.

"Because you know everything, normally," said Luke.

They both looked at the wing carefully and to their astonishment, they realised that the wing had the same markings as the middle mushroom; two circles and one triangle. Even the colour blue was the same. Both children felt that this wing should be put somewhere safe so it would not get damaged. This would then give them time to do some research of their own. This was no cabbage butterfly wing or any other butterfly. Whoever or whatever had lost the wing knew something about those mushrooms. Sophie and Luke both felt there was a connection, in some way.

"What can we put it in?" Sophie asked Luke.

"How about a matchbox? It should fit," Luke replied. "Mum has one of those extra-large boxes on the shelf above the fireplace at home. I'll run back and get it."

Before Sophie could reply, Luke had left the garden and disappeared (similar to the tape measure incident earlier that day).

The wing was still sitting on the top of the middle mushroom, blowing very gently in the breeze. A voice seemed to be coming from the yellow row of daffodils to her left. A gentle voice calling, "Sophie. Sophie."

Who could be calling Sophie when there was no-one there?

"Don't fear my voice, I'm here, behind the daffodils."

Sophie wished with all her heart that Luke would appear and tell her not to be so stupid. But Luke was nowhere to be seen.

"Sophie, Sophie," she heard again.

Suddenly, feeling brave, Sophie slowly walked towards the yellow daffodils. Then, she noticed an identical wing sticking out from behind the daffodil's head. The same as the one still sitting on the middle mushroom. It too, was gently moving with the breeze, but Sophie would be finding out that this one was attached to a fairy called Flueller, the queen of the fairy world. But without her second wing, she could no longer play the role. She would go back to being just another fairy with two plain and normal wings. All her speed was lost while flying and her fairy dust had lost its power too, so she must get her wing back, even if it meant communicating with the humans.

"Sophie, Sophie," she called again.

"Excuse me," replied Sophie very bravely. "How do you know my name?"

"I know everyone's name," answered Flueller very gently. Sophie felt no fear now as she walked very gently towards the daffodils. It was then that she noticed a tiny little face appearing from behind the yellow daffodil, no larger than a one-pence piece. The face was so pretty and so kind.

"Who are you?" asked Sophie.

"My name is Flueller, please give me the wing, I have no use without it."

Sophie could see that the little face was becoming quite sad and Sophie knew that she must give it back to make the face happy again. It was at that very moment that Luke came back into the garden with an almighty dash. The face disappeared as Luke appeared, exhausted and out of breath from running.

"Here, I have found one," he said.

"So have I," replied Sophie. "But now, it's gone."

"Found what?" Luke asked.

"I don't know, it was a face and it spoke to me from behind that daffodil, it wanted its wing back."

"So what did it say?" asked Luke.

"Well, it knew my name and everyone's, Luke."

"You're not making this up, are you, Sophie?" asked Luke.

"Of course not," replied Sophie, "it was there."

"Well, it's not now," replied Luke, picking up the wing gently and placing it in the matchbox. "Let's take it down to the shed and put it in a safe place."

Sophie took one more look behind at the flowers. There was nothing and no trace of anything could be found, so she followed Luke back down the garden to the shed.

Underneath Mr Barker's workbench was an old toolbox which he never used. This was where they left the wing, safely tucked away.

By the time they had finished, it was time to go to bed and Luke started to walk back to his house before dusk. He had a lot to think about. Did Sophie really see a face behind the flowers? And if she did, what was it and who was it? So many questions and no answers. Was this the connection to the mushrooms? Perhaps the so-called face would know about the mushrooms and why they only grew at night. Luke was very tired when he got back home, a little late, but luckily, he was not grounded.

Flueller knew that the coast was clear and the children had gone. The garden was still and quiet when she tiptoed out from behind the daffodils again. If only she had seen earlier where the children had taken her wing. It was time to search while they were sleeping. *But where shall I start?* thought Flueller. She gently flapped her wing and started to rise from the damp grass, but it was so much slower with only one wing; every time she tried to gain speed, nothing happened and she was beginning to get very tired and frustrated. She knew that help was needed, and very patiently, she waited for Freddie to bring his family of four rabbits for food and fun. She waited and waited but there was no sign of Freddie anywhere. She had just given up hope when Freddie appeared.

"There you are," said Flueller.

"It's a very long story," replied Freddie. "The wife decided to have extra time sleeping. We were out late last night and got into a conversation with spiky Phil, the hedgehog, interesting chap, don't you think?"

"Listen, Freddie, I need some help," said Flueller anxiously.

"Whatever is wrong?" asked Freddie, "You look dreadful and where is your wing, Flueller?"

"Where indeed?" replied Flueller. "If I don't find it soon, I will lose my fairy cup and my fairy dust will disappear from my hands and all my power will be gone. I must find my wing Freddie, please help, please," begged Flueller.

"Now, hang on a minute," replied Freddie. "How did you lose your wing in the first place?"

"It doesn't matter," said Flueller. "What matters is that I get it back."

"Right, slow down now and tell me the whole story from the start."

So, she began her story from start to finish. How, whilst flying over the brambles at Gate House Farm, she had caught her wing against the tallest bramble and it had slowly drifted down to the ground. When she reached the spot where it fell, it had disappeared, only to be seen again by the children when they found it on top of the largest mushroom.

"So, how did it get there?" asked Freddie with a long yawn.

"Maybe the wind blew it or something," Flueller confessed, but she had no idea how it reached the mushroom in Sophie's garden.

"Okay," Freddie replied. "Before the rest of the family appear for supper, let's have a search around."

So, that was what they did for at least twenty minutes, but no wing was to be found.

"Excuse me," said Mrs Bunny. "There are hungry mouths to feed here you know, Freddie."

"Yes, okay. I am coming."

And with that, Freddie disappeared. Flueller, at this stage, was feeling very tired and knew that it was time to rest, so she disappeared into the garden, which was very quiet and still once again.

Sophie could not go off to sleep that night thinking about the little face and the voice behind the daffodil calling to her. Getting out of her bed and tiptoeing over to the window, she opened it quietly. The garden was quiet and still but, as always, Sophie could see the mushrooms growing very slowly before her. Tomorrow, they must be measured before they forgot again. Sophie was very tired and closing the window, she climbed back into her bed. There had been lots of changes in the garden today; the sad face and gentle voice behind the daffodils, the mushrooms growing now through the day as well as the night and the little wing which the sad fairy was indeed anxious to have back. *Tomorrow we must find the fairy and give back the wing*, thought Sophie, *and Luke had better agree to that otherwise,* thought Sophie, *I will ban him from my garden.* And Sophie knew that she would, too.

It was Saturday, which was a great bonus for the two children's plans. Sophie was up and dressed by 7:30 am. Luke must have known, as he too, was up and dressed at the same time. The sun was out too and there was a feeling that the day would turn out to be warm and dry, which again, would also help their plans. Luke arrived at Sophie's house just after 7:45 am as he was anxious to find this so-called face of Sophie's and to measure the mushrooms. The night before, Mrs Barker, Sophie's mother, had felt that she should hunt around the house for the tape measure, as she knew how much Sophie loved measuring the fish down the pond. Luckily for the children, she did find it tucked behind a vase at the bottom of the stairs.

"Here we are," she said, as she saw both children disappear into the back garden.

"Thanks, Mum." Sophie took the tape measure and gave her mother a large hug.

"Now remember," Mrs Barker replied, "your party is at 3:30 pm and we have to go shopping for a present too."

"Oh, brother," Sophie said under her breath. Mrs Barker had heard her remark.

"Don't you want to go?" she asked.

"It's not that, Mum, I have so much to do."

"You have plenty of time," replied Mrs Barker, as she raced off to find her duster. *Where on earth did I leave it?* thought Mrs Barker.

Knowing their time was limited, they both ran very fast down to the bottom of the garden, the tape measure safely in Sophie's hand. They arrived at the mushrooms and Luke took the tape measure from Sophie's hand. Both the smaller mushrooms measured the same size, but on measuring the middle mushroom, there was again a difference, it was one inch bigger than yesterday. The most interesting change was how the grass had grown in front of the three mushrooms. So tall that, on looking from the house, the mushrooms could not be seen at all.

"Good," said Luke, "maybe now we can keep the secret from your parents, Sophie. It would be bad if your father chopped them down with the lawnmower."

It was almost like the grass had grown for this purpose in front of the three mushrooms.

"Let's start looking for that face," Luke said with excitement in his voice.

"Well, behind those daffodils would be a good place to start," Sophie replied.

Flueller, the queen of the fairy world, was nowhere to be seen because she was below the ground, asleep. The night before, she had spent many hours looking for her wing, but of course, it was safe in the matchbox in the shed, if only she knew. Luke and Sophie searched everywhere but found nothing.

"This is a waste of time," said Luke, "I don't believe you anymore, Sophie, you made it up."

Sophie was very upset about Luke's remark.

"Tough, then," she said feeling very grown-up, "I am going in to watch TV."

She walked back down the garden, disappearing into the house. Luke wandered back in the garden and it was then that the idea appeared in his head. He would get the wing out of the matchbox and place it back on the middle mushroom. *Maybe, just maybe, the face would see it and appear to reclaim the wing, then we shall see,* thought Luke, so that was what he did. The wing was placed very carefully on the middle mushroom. Luckily, the day was still with no wind to blow the wing away, so he waited and waited, but there was no sign of the sad face. He waited for at least one hour. Luke never thought, in a million years, that he could keep so still and quiet, but he did.

Flueller could not rest at all. All she could think about was her lack of power when flying and her lack of fairy dust. She must find her wing and quickly, before the others found out about it. So, she stretched and yawned. Flueller's home was under the mushrooms. To reach her level, she had to go through a small entrance in the stalk of the middle mushroom, not difficult for Flueller as it was only two inches high, then a long green slide down to her bed of petals, where she could sleep and rest for a million years if she wanted to, but now was not the time to sleep and rest. Although her body wanted to, her mind would not sleep until her wing was found above the ground. Brushing herself down from her petal bed, she lifted her feet from the ground and slowly fluttered to the surface. Much slower, of course, as she now only had one wing. Opening the small door to the entrance, she returned once again into the outside world. Adjusting to the light, not realising Luke was in the garden hiding, Flueller moved away from the security of the mushrooms. Suddenly, she noticed her wing on top of the middle mushroom and the sadness left her face as she picked it up. *Freddie must have found it for me, how very kind,* she thought. She would be sending him some special fairy dust when she had the time. Her job now was to return to her home under the ground to repair her damaged wing. Luke had been very patient and this was his reward. He was very nervous at this point, never before had he seen a real fairy, and probably never would again, he thought. But now, he was anxious to know more, especially where she lived, how she had lost her wing and what did she do with all his teeth when she took them. Maybe it was a true story, after all. Quickly, before he lost his nerve, he called out to Flueller.

"Are you a real fairy?"

It was all he could think of at that moment. Flueller had no time to open the door and disappear. Rather than appear to be rude, she answered Luke.

"Yes, I am a real fairy and my name is Flueller and yours is Luke," she said to Luke very bravely. *These folk on the outside were not to be trusted,* she thought to herself.

"I'm glad you have your wing back," replied Luke. "How did you know my name?"

"I must go now and repair my wing, I need to fly again soon," said Flueller, and with that, she disappeared through the little door and down the slide, made from a very strong root.

Luke was so surprised at how quickly the little fairy disappeared, and very anxiously now, he walked towards the middle mushroom searching for the entrance where the little fairy had left, but what Luke did not realise was that he needed a secret word to open the little door. He could see the door slightly below the surface of the ground. Half of the entrance was in view while the rest was below. Luke realised that when he touched the entrance; he could feel the heat on his hands and a strange humming sound. He needed to get through this doorway to see what was on the opposite side. Regardless of pushing and pulling, nothing opened the door, but then nothing would, except the magic word. No one knew this except Flueller, and Flueller had gone through the door so he could not ask her.

"Luke, guess what's on the TV," called Sophie from the house.

"I'm not interested," Luke replied back.

He's sulking, thought Sophie, *oh well, let him miss it,* thought Sophie again. Sophie went back into the house and left Luke in the garden. Luke realised that there was nothing more he could do in the garden today. The mushrooms had been measured and he had met the sad face, which now appeared to be a fairy. Suddenly, he felt a drop of rain on his hand, looking up, he realised how grey the sky had become. *Maybe it is time to go and watch some TV with Sophie. She will only sulk,* thought Luke, so he left the mushrooms and returned to Sophie's house, anxious and very eager to tell her about the doorway and the little fairy.

"I'm not listening," said Sophie.

"Up to you," replied Luke, "you won't be coming with me then, will you?"

"Maybe," said Sophie.

"Then you do believe me," Luke replied.

"I said, maybe," Sophie replied again. They both burst out laughing, each grabbing a packet of crisps from the kitchen cupboard; how excited the children felt. *What a special day this has been. Even better than the party later*, thought Sophie.

The rain stopped as quickly as it had started and the grey cloud disappeared and a white cloud appeared, and then the sky filled with blue and the sun came out. It was going to be a nice day as well as an exciting one. Flueller had no one to help her repair her wing. All her family and friends had disappeared when the Tabots had returned on that awful night she would never forget. Maybe, just maybe, her family would return one day. Meanwhile, she must repair her wing and the only way she knew would be full of danger. Flueller knew that without her wing, she would eventually die and her quality of life would die too. She must make a decision, and just maybe, Luke and Sophie could help her. So, with her decision made, she settled down to her soft bed for a sleep which she felt she really deserved, with a nettle tea to follow. She would then return to the surface hoping the children were still in the garden.

Getting bored with the TV, Luke and Sophie decided to return to the garden to try to open the little door below the middle mushroom. The grass was a little damp from the rain earlier. As the two children walked down to the mushrooms at the bottom of the garden, Sophie felt excited at the thought of seeing the fairy and the entrance to the doorway.

"See, I told you so," Luke said with excitement in his voice. Sophie could see it too, but there was no sign of the fairy.

"Let's hide and wait," Luke said, "it worked the last time."

So, that was what they did, just like before when Luke had hid quietly. As time stood still below the ground, Flueller slept for a rather long time, but when she awoke, she reached for her nettle tea, which was waiting for her at just the right temperature. Her thoughts were with the children and how she would ask them for their help. Leaving her wing in a safe place, she fluttered up to the doorway and walked through. Once on the surface, she looked around the garden with caution; empty and quiet, no sign of the children. *Time to be brave and call their names. So, here goes,* thought Flueller.

"Luke? Sophie? Are you there?" she called.

The children could not believe it. The little voice was back, calling to them both.

"What do we do now?" whispered Sophie.

"Go for it," replied Luke.

So, very quietly, they walked out of their safe hiding place behind the oak tree. Flueller saw the children and knew that they would help her now. She tiptoed out from behind the daffodils once again.

"Will you help me?" she asked the children.

"Yes," they replied together, "of course."

They both knew that they had found a special friendship with Flueller. What they did not know was that they were on the first part of a journey. Level Control was about to begin for them and level one was where it started.

Chapter Two
Level One

Taking a seat on the smaller of the three mushrooms, while the children sat on the grass, Flueller started her story. She told the children about how she had lost her wing in the first place and how the only way to repair her wing was to take them down below the ground to level one. This would involve searching for Boris, the evil spider, and on finding his cobweb, they would take just a little of the special thread, which is known to the fairies as a remedy to mend their wings. This would have to be done while the spider was out hunting. They also had to find his web on level one.

"This is not just an adventure for you, children," said Flueller, with concern in her little gentle voice. "You will be in great danger, and not just from Boris. At all times, we must stay together and never leave the chosen route. If you do, you will never return and this would be fatal for you and your families."

Luke looked at Sophie with great concern on his face, Sophie looked at Luke, feeling very frightened after listening to Flueller's words.

"Well," said Flueller, "will you still help me now?"

The children knew what the risks would be but they felt so sure that their help was needed.

"We have to help you," Luke replied.

"Yes," said Sophie, "we do."

With that, Flueller nodded and said the magic word which would open the doorway to her world.

"Marvellous!" she said loudly, and with that, an opening appeared, large enough for the children to enter. Flueller walked through first while Luke followed and then Sophie. The door closed behind them.

"Firstly, I will show you my home and collect my wing for repair," said Flueller in earnest. With that said, she disappeared very quickly down the root of the mushroom to her bed below. The children looked on with great excitement, for before them was a slippery green root.

"It's a slide," said Luke, "This is going to be fun."

With that, he too disappeared before Sophie's eyes, leaving Sophie totally on her own, but as Luke had felt earlier, Sophie was feeling heat and a humming noise coming from below her feet.

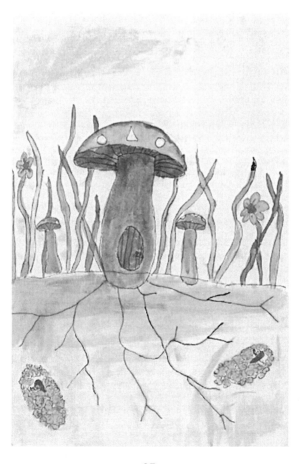

Feeling very scared, Sophie stepped onto the top of the root. It was very slippery and she knew that instead of sitting up, she would have to lie down to reach the bottom and that is exactly what she did. No sooner had she laid herself down that she was sliding very fast down the root into a very soft floor below her feet because she was so scared at the top; her eyes were still closed. She could feel the softness below her feet. *I hope it's all like this,* Sophie thought.

"Open your eyes now," she heard Flueller say.

"That was fun," she heard Luke say.

Opening her eyes, Sophie realised what she was standing on. Yellow petals were all around her feet. The smell was similar to roses, although they looked nothing like them.

"This is where I sleep," Flueller said, quite excited that they both liked her bed so much. "It's safe here."

"Safe from what?" asked Luke.

"Boris, the spider, even worse than Boris," replied Flueller, with a very worried look on her gentle little face, "the Tabots were here and my family is now gone, taken by Draydon several months ago."

Sophie looked at Luke and then back at Flueller.

"But why?" she asked Flueller, "What did they do?"

"My mother was queen of the fairy world, father the king, he went missing before mother, no one knows where. Mother was concerned that there was no return. She went out to look for him and she too did not return. Next day, the Tabots came and took the rest of my family. Now, I search for them, day and night, while the heat becomes hotter and the humming louder."

"But what is that noise and why is it getting hotter?" Luke asked Flueller.

"The underworld has many levels of energies, each one stronger than the last. I believe my family has gone to the lowest level in the ground but this level has the highest energy of all and the most dangerous too. I believe that they are using my parents' energy to create more power at the lowest level. They plan to take this power of energy into your world. The

Tabots will then control not only the underworld but your world too."

With that, a large tear appeared, rolling down Flueller's cheeks.

"Please don't cry," said Sophie, very sadly.

"We will help you get your family back, won't we, Luke?"

Bravely, Luke agreed. Realising now that not only was Boris the spider, their enemy, but also a bunch of Tabots.

"What do they look like?" he asked, "these Tabots?"

"If I tell you, you will go back to your world," said Flueller. And both children knew they would. "So, do you still want to help me?" asked Flueller.

Luke looked at Sophie.

"Can we talk about this, please?" she asked Luke.

Flueller fluttered past them both, leaving them to talk in private.

"I'm scared, Luke, are you?"

"Yes," replied Luke, with concern on his face.

"But, Sophie, we have to help Flueller, she has no one else."

"Yes, I know but…"

"No butting, Sophie, go home if you must, this is far more exciting than a stupid party anyway."

Sophie thought about what Luke had said, maybe he was right, it could be more exciting. Flueller reappeared with concern on her face.

"Well," she said, "will you help me?"

"Yes," they both said together.

Flueller clapped her hands. "Thank you, children," she said, with excitement back in her voice, "I knew you were special as soon as I saw you. Now, here's my wing, let's go find Boris's web before it gets too hot and noisy."

So, they all left the security of Flueller's home, lifting some petals from her bed, Luke and Sophie saw the second entrance which they were about to enter. Flueller did not say a magic word for this one. It opened automatically.

"Off we all go," she said to them, and with her wing firmly in her little hand, they started their journey. With every step they took, they could feel the heat getting hotter and hotter and the humming becoming louder and louder. It was how the Tabots communicated. Flueller knew they were getting nearer all the time but she kept this quiet from the two children. Nothing must stop them now. The doorway opened up into a long, dark tunnel and the children could hear water running at this stage of the journey, although, nothing could be seen. Both of them thought it was too soon to ask too many questions, so keeping quiet, they moved on.

Although it was very dark, they could still see a little. The air was very clammy and dry as the heat seemed to be increasing. With each step that they took, they knew they were getting nearer and nearer to danger. *Perhaps the party was a better idea after all,* thought Sophie. The tunnel never seemed to end and at last, they could sense more light appearing.

"Once through this tunnel," Flueller said, "You must be aware that we are entering the territory where Boris lives. He will strike very quickly at his prey; there can be no escape. We must be very quiet and walk very quickly through the next tunnel."

Not another one, thought Luke. The second tunnel seemed even longer than the first, which made Luke and Sophie feel a little less frightened. The tunnel finally ended and they were now entering an area of grassland, no trees could be seen.

Nothing but very long grass. But Luke and Sophie had never seen such long grass before. Even the grass that had been growing around their mushrooms seemed very short compared to this. It was still very hot and the humming could still be heard.

"Be careful now," whispered Flueller, "Boris could be anywhere."

"Great," replied Luke, "we are his free dinner."

"Shut up!" replied Sophie. So, he did.

Still clutching the tiny wing, Flueller quietly led the way. With each step, she could feel more energy slipping away from her. The web had to be found quickly. So far, there was no sign of the spider amongst the tall grass.

Sophie started to become very itchy, she had very sensitive skin and this grass was doing her no favours. It was then that they noticed the huge cobweb, suspended from a large, thick bush. The smell was unbelievable. The two children had never smelt anything like it before. It was like a cross between a smelly old dustbin and a pile of horse manure, with a drop of Mum's old perm lotion thrown in. Sophie got her tissue out from her jeans pocket while Luke had nothing but his sweatshirt to cover his nose.

"I'm used to it," Flueller said.

"No one on earth could be used to that," replied Sophie.

Flueller giggled and Luke started laughing too.

"My cousin's nappy smells better than this," he said, wrapping his sweatshirt even tighter around his nose.

"I bet," said Sophie, "grow up."

Little did Sophie know that they were now in the field of suggestions and what they suggested was a dangerous thing to do. But the children had no idea of this and to Sophie's amazement, Luke started to grow up and up and up, into the long blades of grass, until his head was touching the top and he could see for miles, which was quite a bonus.

"What do you see?" Flueller asked Luke.

"Miles and miles of grass," Luke replied.

Relieved that Boris was nowhere to be seen, Luke then realised how tall he had grown.

"What do I do, Flueller?" he asked anxiously.

"You stay up there," replied Flueller.

"You will be useful for a lookout. Don't worry, when we make another suggestion, you will come down."

Luke felt reassured about this and felt very proud that he was so tall; it allowed him to do the job. Meanwhile, down below in the grass, Flueller and Sophie were looking at the giant cobweb in front of them. Sophie had never seen anything like it in her life and probably never would again. If it had not been so smelly, she would have found the cobweb far more beautiful. The smell was too overpowering, making

31

Sophie feel sick. So was the thought of meeting this so-called spider, Boris.

Luke was feeling very proud of his new job as the watchman. He felt that he was safe above the top of the grass but little did he realise how wrong he would be. Flueller was now becoming more anxious by the second. She was used to the stench coming from the giant cobweb but she would need Sophie's help in cutting a thread from the web. This needed to be done quickly, before the Spider returned from his hunting.

"We must move fast, Sophie," said Flueller with a very worried look on her face.

"But how do we cut the web? It looks rather strong," said Sophie.

"With that," said Flueller, "Let this blade of grass cut the web."

And it did. Taking the blade of grass from its roots, Flueller carefully cut a thread from the enormous web, very careful not to cut her fingers or the other fixed on her delicate shoulders.

"There," she said, "we have it good."

Putting it together with the piece of thread, she moved away from the web, feeling very proud of her efforts. Luke was feeling tired now. The light seemed to be fading fast and his eyes were feeling very tired from watching for the spider. One more scan around the field and that was it; his job was done and he was now anxious to get back to his normal size. He looked to his left, all clear, then his right, still all clear. He also looked behind him and everything appeared clear. Suddenly, to his horror, coming straight for him, was the worst nightmare of his life. The biggest spider he had ever seen. It seemed to be heading straight for him, eager to receive his prey.

"Help, get me down!" Luke cried out loud.

Flueller knew instantly what was heading straight for them. Keeping as calm as she could for the children's sake, she returned Luke's call.

"Listen, Luke, do as I say. 'I want to be my normal size again' say it, Luke, say it now."

But Luke was so scared, his voice had disappeared.

"What's wrong?" Flueller called, but of course, Luke could not reply because he had no voice. "Say it, Luke, say it before it's all too late."

Closer and closer came the spider, eager for his dinner, which appeared to be a starter, the main meal, and the pudding, as he scanned the field and spotted Flueller and Sophie.

"Listen, Luke, can you hear me?" Flueller said with great concern in her now very anxious voice. "You must stay calm. Boris can sense the way you are feeling and he will know that there will be no hunting to do; you will play straight into his plans. Now, be very still and quiet and listen to me."

And with that, she explained to Luke how much further away Boris was. Although it looked like he was close, she also quickly explained to Luke that they had one more suggestion before they ran out. As the rule of the underworld was just three, they must get this one right.

"I want to go home," said Sophie, "I hate spiders. Please send it away."

Flueller knew that this was an impossible task as she was growing weaker with every minute.

"We must all stay very calm. Now, listen, Luke, say after me, 'shrink me down to my normal size.'"

She also reminded him that there were no more suggestions left so no more mistakes must be made, otherwise, Luke would be dinner for Boris and maybe the others too. Luke sensed how important this was, focusing again on the large spider coming straight for him, but above the grass; the humming he had heard earlier that day seemed to be so much louder and the heat so much hotter.

"I can't hear you, Flueller. I can't hear you."

Hearing this comment from Luke, Flueller acted quickly. If there was a spare suggestion she could use, she knew what she would ask and that would be for the humming to stop for a moment, just a few seconds would have been enough. Thinking quickly, she knew what had to be done.

"Sophie, you see this blade of grass? You must hold it steady while I begin my climb."

"But what about me?" Sophie replied.

"Just hold the blade of grass steady, it's okay, we will all be fine if you do as I say." With that said, Sophie knew that she must do as she was told.

Holding the blade of grass very carefully in both her hands, Flueller slowly made the climb to the top, maybe then Luke would hear her voice above the loud humming. As she was so weak, it seemed a very long time before she reached the top.

"Help! Help!" she heard Luke shouting from the top of the grass. Flueller was feeling weaker and weaker with every step she climbed, so much so that she nearly fell three times off of the blade of grass. She also knew how sharp the blade was and several times, she nearly cut herself. Luke tried to believe that the spider was miles and miles away; he kept saying this over and over in his mind. Suddenly, he realised that Flueller was looking at him from the top of the blade of grass. Flueller could see the relief on Luke's face.

"Now, listen," she said, "there is no time left, you must ask for what you want right at this moment, more than anything else in the world and I must not tell you as the suggestion will then be mine and not yours. Do you understand, Luke?"

"Yes," said Luke, "I do."

Flueller started the return journey down the blade of grass as Luke decided in his head what to suggest so that there were no mistakes made. Once safely down to the ground, Flueller and Sophie waited, hoping that Luke now understood just what he had to do. Boris scanned the scene once more; he could see Luke and he knew that there were two more bodies on the ground. Boris had not eaten for several days and he was very hungry. Closer and closer he got to his prey; his mouth was ready and his many legs were active and ready to grab his victim and the two others on the ground. Luke was now ready to ask for his suggestion, knowing that one silly mistake, and their lives would be over.

"Let me be my normal size again," he requested.

He immediately felt a strange sensation as he started to shrink and as quickly as he had grown, he was shrinking, back to his normal size.

Once Luke was on the ground, Flueller reminded them both there was no time for a reunion, as they were still in very grave danger. Boris was still hunting for them and they needed to move very quickly.

"You must both run as fast as you can in that direction," Flueller cried.

"But what about you?" asked Luke, "You saved my life, now we must stay together and protect you."

"Yes, we must, you are our friend." Sophie replied.

"You can run fast, children, I will be slower but do not fret as I have been chased by Boris before and I know his pace and the tricks which he uses. Now, run like the wind and I will see you on the next level."

With that, Flueller disappeared, leaving the children all alone.

"We have to do as she says," said Luke, "And hope that we will see her on the next level."

Luke noticed that Sophie had a large tear falling down her cheek.

"Don't worry, she will be okay. Remember, she is a fairy."

Luke grabbed Sophie's hand, and together, they ran in the direction that Flueller had pointed to.

Sophie hated running, she had always been useless at it, whereas Luke was a keen footballer, so it was very easy for him.

"Come on, Sophie, do you really want to be Boris's dinner?"

Enough said, and with that, Sophie ran with all her might, never before had she ran so fast, but Boris could run very fast too, faster than the two children and he was far, far wiser. He knew the direction that Flueller had sent them and he reached this a long time before Luke and Sophie did. He waited very patiently, a trick that he was very good at, having no idea that the massive spider was hiding ahead of them.

"I think we have lost the stupid spider, Sophie."

"How do ·you know that?" Sophie replied.

"I just do, we have been running a long time now and I can't see him. Can you?"

"No," Sophie replied.

They were both feeling very tired as they both sat down on the warm ground. They were also feeling very hungry; so much had happened that the children had not even thought about this. Boris was very hungry but he was not tired, he hunted for hours at a time and this had been an easy day for him so far.

Luke and Sophie were so sleepy and their eyes were feeling very heavy. It was so difficult to keep them open. Sophie felt the grass irritating her again as she brushed it from her arms, but this was no blade of grass. Luke realised that a long black spider's leg was resting on Sophie's arm and he then knew that the spider had got there before them. He knew that if he said anything to Sophie she would flip and it would all be over. Trying to appear calm, he made a joke about how bad Sophie was at sports. Boris was keeping very still, he had spotted his worst enemy, Bellray, the snake. He knew that the children were resting below him. If he made a sudden move, Bellray would spot him and he would then become his dinner. This was the best thing that could have happened to Luke and Sophie. They could take the chance and run again, so this is what they did. Sophie pushed Boris's leg away from her arm, she had no idea it was anything else but a blade of grass, and once again, they ran as fast as they could. Boris could see them and he had to make a quick decision before he lost his opportunity to strike, but it was too late, Bellray, the giant snake, had spotted him and he was now ready to strike and poor Boris never stood a chance. That was the end of his hunting days. The humming was so much louder now that the children did not hear all the sounds as the huge snake enjoyed his supper.

Luke and Sophie never once looked back, they just kept running with all the energy they had left. Luke was coping with this better than Sophie. Her legs felt like jelly and every bone in her body ached. She had never felt worse, even when she had her tonsils out and that, she felt, was bad enough.

"Keep running, Sophie, don't look back."

Sophie knew that for once, she must listen to Luke's words.

Bellray was still very hungry, giant spiders did not seem to satisfy him these days. *Maybe one would have helped,* he thought, *or even three, but the taste could get boring. What else could be on his menu?* He thought this over for a few minutes and then it dawned on him; the other two. *Now, where are they?* he thought. Bellray uncurled his huge yellow body. He lifted his huge head high above the grass and looked around the field. It was then he spotted his target. Above his bloodshot eyes, he raised his extra two scanner-vision eyes, this would enable him to view the field for many more miles, and it worked, for there they were, two miles ahead. Although Luke had ordered Sophie not to look back, he was doing just the opposite and now he wished that he had not for what he saw seemed even worse than Boris. The huge snake was about six miles tall, although maybe it seemed that long to Luke as it had a huge spiky mane. Luke thought it looked like an enormous snake and a little like a sea serpent, although it was yellow in colour. Luke could see it very clearly in the grass as it was moving very fast and rather than sliding, as a snake would do, it seemed to be gliding above the ground, towards the two children. He knew that they were in just as much danger as they were when Boris appeared. *In fact*, he thought, *even more, as this creature seemed to be moving far quicker than the giant spider. Where is Boris? If he turned up, how much worse would this all be then?* Bellray could see on his scan of vision that Luke had spotted him.

"Run!" he shouted, "you can run but there is nowhere to hide." And with that said, he let out a very loud laugh which echoed across the field of grass. Luke and Sophie held their hands to both their ears as piercing pain shot through their heads and seemed to stop them both in their tracks. Bellray knew just what to do as he gained speed; two miles was nothing to him. As the children laid motionless on the ground, he was on top of them both in seconds, raising his large head and showing his sharp fangs. The sound produced by Bellray had stopped Luke and Sophie in their tracks, they could not move any part of their bodies. Bellray had made a mistake, not only had the children heard the sound from Bellray but Stellight, a powerful little goblin, had heard it too. At last, it was payback time for Stellight.

Bellray had hunted and eaten too many of Stellight's friends. He knew nothing about the two children, but there was a very good reason that they were here and one of those reasons was now staring him in the face. He was not afraid of Bellray and Bellray knew it too, he also knew that Stellight was a powerful goblin of the highest order. Bellray had fed on many of his friends over the years and he also sensed that this was payback time. Bellray started to panic and smiling at the little goblin, he said, "Why don't you just let me go quietly?"

"You dare to ask me to let you go?" replied Stellight. "After what you have done to my friends?"

"I am only a humble snake who has a large appetite now and again," he replied.

"A large appetite, you could call it that, Bellray, but I call it greed and stupidity on your part. Did you really think you would keep getting away with it?" asked Stellight, with interest.

Bellray knew that his life depended on the right answer. Since the Tabots had come, food had been scarce on this level.

"I have been too scared to move on to level two," Bellray replied, believing that this would be a good enough answer for Stellight, then he could go on his way and find some more food, even if it was just another goblin, or maybe two.

"Think carefully," Stellight said, "I can read your every thought, you stupid creature."

Bellray could sense that the goblin's tone was changing. In his next breath, Bellray said, "I promise that I will never eat another goblin," but in his mind, he was saying, *if you were fatter, you stupid goblin, I would hunt you down and eat you very slowly.*

"Bad move," shouted Stellight at the top of his voice and with that said, the huge snake disappeared, never to return. Stellight was so glad to see the back of Bellray, as over the years, he had caused a lot of anger on level one, believing that he was the fastest hunter on this level, but Stellight knew different. Observing the two children, he raised both his hands to the sky above.

"Larmayor," he said.

The children started to yawn very loudly; they felt as if they had been asleep for a very long time. As they both started to focus once again, they noticed a little goblin sitting on the ground in front of them. Luke knew that this little man was a good person and he looked at Sophie, who was taking a little longer to come round.

"He's okay, don't be scared," Luke said.

Sophie smiled at the little goblin; she felt a good energy from him too.

"What is your name?" asked Luke.

Stellight crossed his arms and legs, he seemed to be getting in a comfortable position, before he answered Luke.

"My name is Stellight and I am a goblin from the first noman. I understand from Flueller that you kindly helped her with her wing, our mushrooms are in your garden back home and this tells me that you are both special beings and the chosen ones."

"What do you mean by chosen ones?" asked Luke.

"It's a very long story, children, firstly, we need to eat and then I will tell you more."

The children were very excited about the thought of eating as they were now both very thirsty and hungry. "Good, then we will eat."

Now, Stellight was very a powerful goblin, whatever he visualised would appear, but he also knew the power of the children, so he would teach them the art of positive thinking and visualisation.

"What would you like to eat?" he said to them both.

"Fish and chips with bread and butter," Luke said.

"And how about Sophie?" asked Stellight.

Sophie thought for a moment, "In my head, I can see a large strawberry milkshake and a cheeseburger covered in tomato sauce."

And with that said, it appeared in front of Sophie just as she had visualised it.

"Hang on a minute," Luke said, "How come you have your food and mine is still not here?"

Stellight then asked Sophie what she had done before her food had arrived.

"Nothing, except think about it in my head."

"There is your answer, Luke," replied Stellight.

"How easy is that?" said Luke.

He quickly started thinking about a large plate of fish and chips, and there it was, in seconds, cooked and prepared just as he liked it.

"Thank you so much, Stellright."

"I think you have that wrong," Sophie chanted. "It's *Stellight* not *Stellright.*"

Luke felt very embarrassed at getting the goblin's name wrong, especially as he had been so kind with the food and saving their lives earlier.

"Don't worry," said Stellight. "You will soon remember it."

They started to tuck into their food; it was every bit as good as it looked.

"What do you eat?" asked Sophie, as she wiped a large piece of ketchup from her mouth.

"I only eat twice a year when the rest of the noman meet."

"Don't you get hungry in between?" asked Luke with interest.

"You must understand we are not of the human form, food is not our main source of energy, but as you have asked, I will join you in your feast."

He visualised his choice and it appeared just as the other food had done.

"Yuck!" Sophie said, loudly, "It looks horrid."

In front of Stellight was a plate filled with long things which looked a little like pasta, if only it was, for as the children looked more carefully at the plate, they realised that the pasta was moving around the plate.

"Oh my god," said Luke with horror on his face.

"Don't worry, it's not as bad as it looks."

"But what is it?" Luke asked Stellight.

"They are called puck worms, they have to be eaten straight away otherwise they chase each other around the plate, they then lose all their energy, leaving no energy left for me when I eat them."

He started to gobble them up by scooping them in his hands as fast as he could. The children had never seen anything like it before in their lives. Within seconds, Stellight had cleared the plate.

"Yum," he said.

Luke and Sophie felt that they had better change the subject concerning Stellight's eating habits. As they enjoyed the rest of their food, Sophie started to think about her home and her mum and dad and then she started to think about how long they must have now been gone. Their parents must be getting frantic above the mushrooms.

"I know what you are thinking, Sophie," Stellight said. "But don't worry unnecessarily. Your parents know nothing about your adventures while you are down here, time will be standing still in your world."

The two children both looked at each other in amazement.

"Do you mean that…" asked Luke.

"Of course, Luke, a goblin never tells lies."

"Wicked," said Luke.

"Why is that wicked?" replied Stellight, "I thought that it would stop them from worrying where you had disappeared to."

Luke started laughing and then he thought it would be rude not to explain to Stellight what he had meant by his figure of speech. They all started laughing after that. Remembering about Boris, the spider, Luke started asking Stellight where he had gone but Stellight did not think it was necessary to explain. The children understood and they thanked the goblin once again for saving their lives and for the lovely meals. Their stomachs were full and it was time to rest. Stellight reassured them both that there was no danger and he would be a lookout for them while they were sleeping. Trusting his words, the children made themselves comfortable on the ground and seconds later, they were both asleep. Stellight remained awake, just as he had promised. Daylight came far too soon for the two children, as they stretched and opened their eyes, but Stellight was nowhere to be seen and they realised that they were back on their own.

"Why did he have to go?" Sophie cried.

"Perhaps we will see him again on the next level when we meet Flueller."

"Do you believe that we will?" Sophie asked.

"We have to believe them both."

"Yes," said Sophie, "we do."

They began to wake up more fully, and standing on their feet, they both brushed themselves down. At first, they thought they were covered in grass, but on looking more carefully, they realised that it was no grass. All their bare skin was covered in brown fur and they then began to realise how cold the temperature was. It must have been the last thing that Stellight had done before he had disappeared, preparing them for the next level. The temperature was below zero and they would need protection from it; they both now knew how a big brown bear must feel.

"Thank you," Sophie shouted out loud.

"Yes, thank you, Stellight."

In the far distance, they could hear Stellight's voice.

"Thank you, Luke. Thank you, Sophie," he cried.

The two children were feeling a little sad now that Stellight had gone but they sensed that there was no time to become broody. They both remembered the direction that they had been running before Flueller had disappeared and off they went. The long grass seemed to be clearing as they carried on walking. The temperature seemed to be dropping very quickly, Luke and Sophie were so relieved to have the warm fur against their skin and luckily, Sophie did not appear to be sensitive towards it. Very soon, they reached the end of the field and stopping in their tracks, they looked at each other for some answers on where to go next, no doorways appeared, no helpful goblins, nothing.

"What are we going to do?" said Sophie to Luke.

"Let's just wait and see," Luke answered. And that was what they did. Only, nothing happened and no one appeared.

"Do you remember the magic word that Flueller used to open the first doorway?"

"I haven't a clue," Sophie replied.

By now, it was getting very cold, they would have to move fast; they both wanted to be warm again.

"What about another suggestion?" asked Sophie.

"It's too late. Three have been used, remember?" said Luke.

"It's so cold, I hate being cold."

"You hate being hot," replied Luke. "Make up your mind, Sophie."

"It's better than being cold," Sophie said, shivering.

"It's better than being hot. Or is it better than being cold? I like being hot or do I like being cold?"

"Shut up, Luke," Sophie cried.

"I haven't said anything," Luke shouted back.

They then realised that the voice was coming from the ground below. Clearing the grass away, Luke noticed a tiny brown mouse looking up at them both.

"It's cold, it's hot, or is it hot and cold?" the little mouse cried in his squeaky little voice.

When the tiny little mouse realised he had been spotted, he thought now he had gone way too far with his comment. Just as he started to crawl away, Luke grabbed him by the tail, he had no fear of mice so this was very easy for him to do. Holding the mouse in front of him, Luke said, "Can you help us find the doorway to the next level?"

The mouse thought for a moment and then he replied: "Maybe if you have some cheese."

"That's easy," Luke replied.

Just as Stellight had shown them, he focused on a large piece of cheese in his mind and seconds later, the piece of cheese appeared in front of the little mouse. Luke was very proud of himself and Sophie thought how clever he was too; a special piece of cheese for a very special mouse.

"I will tell you when I have eaten it."

"Now, wait a minute," Luke said, "First, you must tell us where the next doorway is."

"Must I?" said the little mouse, "I have been running around this big old field for days and days, let me eat the cheese first and then I will tell you."

Unlike Stellight, Luke and Sophie did not feel that they could trust this little field mouse.

"You tell us first and then you get your cheese, do you understand?" he asked the mouse.

The little mouse thought it over and then he agreed he would tell the children where the next doorway was.

"It's to your left four paces, six paces to your right and then one more pace to your left, twist the blade of grass around once in your hand and then tug it out of the ground. Now, can I have my cheese?" he said. Giving the mouse his cheese, they left him to eat it.

Following his instructions, they started to tug the piece of grass out of the field and realised where the next doorway stood. To their left, they could see the ground opening and some stairs appearing; it was now time to leave level one.

It was so cold that they were eager to enter the next level and as they started to step down the dark staircase, they both felt the brown fur leaving their bodies. As the heat rose, Stellight was looking after them once again. The dark staircase seemed to be getting more and more difficult to descend, each step becoming deeper and deeper, and all the time the air was becoming hotter and hotter, and once again, they could hear the humming sound below their feet.

"I am so hungry," Sophie said.

"We will eat later. First, we must find the next safe person to trust."

"But what if it's another spider, like Boris?" Sophie said anxiously.

"There are no more spiders," Luke replied.

"But how can you be so sure, Luke?" Sophie asked.

"I just am, now save your energy for later, Sophie" Luke replied.

The stairway never seemed to end, but finally, they could feel the last stair, and feeling relieved, they tried to adjust their eyes to the darkness, feeling their way ahead towards the dark wall.

Chapter Three
Level Two

As both children began to adjust to the little light they had, they carried on with their journey. The stairs ended finally.

"Try and focus your eyes, Sophie," Luke said with an element of relief in his voice. "I can see a light ahead, how about you?"

Sophie did as Luke suggested and she too could see the light up ahead. They used this as their guide, instead of Flueller, but they both knew that they would all meet up again, *and the sooner the better*, they both thought. As they stepped forward towards the next level of their journey, they noticed the figure up ahead. Luke held Sophie's hand, they both knew that they would have to make their presence known to this person, whoever they may be.

"I will do the talking," Luke said.

Sophie was quite happy that Luke was taking charge of the situation.

"You must keep hold of my hand, just in case we need to run."

Sophie suddenly felt rather nervous as they walked with caution up to the figure. Standing in front of them, with her back towards them, was a woman dressed in a long blue robe. The colour was very similar to the blue on top of the middle mushroom in their garden. *Maybe,* thought Luke, *there was another connection.* As quiet as they could, they walked towards the figure in blue. Suddenly, the figure turned and stared straight into the children's faces. They could see clearly that it was a woman, her face was full of deep lines and crevices. They were both feeling the same, this woman looked very old, in fact, hundreds of years older than both their nan and grandad. The children could not take their eyes off this very old face. As they carried on staring, they saw much more; her face was completely round with no chin and she appeared to have no nose, which alarmed the children. Although she was staring straight at them, she appeared to not see them.

"Wait here," said Luke.

He started to walk up to the woman, leaving Sophie's side, but Sophie trusted Luke and quietly stood still. The figure had four strands of hair on each side of her head. The children could clearly count the strands and she was completely bald on the top of her very round head. Her eyes were very large, taking up a large amount of her face, her mouth was very small but she seemed to have a smile appearing.

It was at that moment when she first spoke to Luke and Sophie.

"My," she said. "What a brave pair you are, and you being the braver one of the two."

Luke, still feeling very brave, replied, "Do you know where we can find Flueller, the fairy?"

"Why do you think I should know the whereabouts of the fairy?" replied the figure.

"She seems to know many people in the underworld," Luke said.

"I know not of any fairy," the figure replied.

Luke walked to the left of the figure but he noticed that the eyes of the figure stayed quite still.

"I cannot see you but I can feel your presence," she said. Sophie then decided to join in the conversation.

"Have you a name?" she asked the woman in front of them both.

"My name is Clementer, I am the last of the race of bomadas. The Tabots cleared our race from this level, where we were once ruling. They are wicked people, evil, aggressive and mean. They will do anything to rule the underworld and your kingdom above the ground. The day they came for me, the humming became so intense and I could feel their presence, even though I could not see them. They tried to find me for many days but I am a wise old soul, many years older and with much more wisdom. They gave up in the end and left, but I feel sure they will be back. Their mission is far too precious for them not to be."

The children both listened with interest as she continued her story.

"This is where you fit in. If two people from above our world can reach the lowest level, the energy will stop and the Tabots will be destroyed. The moment your human energy reaches the level, peace will once more be restored and many people from this world will be released and their families will return to lead their normal lives once again."

The children then knew how important their jobs were. Clementer stared at them both and smiled again.

"You are the only ones that can save our world, two very special people."

"But you are very special too," Sophie replied.

"Hiding from the Tabots is not a special gift, just a lucky one," Clementer replied.

"Can you come with us?" asked Luke.

Clementer bowed her head. "Unfortunately not, I will not survive if I leave this level."

"Is there anyone who can lead us there?" asked Luke.

"I am not certain, only you will see as you move on to each level. The Tabots have taken many and I have no knowledge of who is left now," she replied, "I can give you no help other than this."

Clementer reached into a deep, deep pocket in her gown and placed a tiny blue triangle into Luke's hand.

"You must remember to activate this when you need guidance and help on the next level. It cannot be used on this level."

"How do we do that?" asked Luke.

"Here, I will show you."

Clementer took the blue triangle from Luke's hands.

"Close your eyes and count to five and speak out loud, 'light and love, send to me light and love for all to see'. This is very powerful and the energy is very intense. Once activated, the power can stay with you for as much as one hour of the day or night. Remember this and never forget, this will be your guiding light and maybe the answer to your journey to the lowest level. Now, repeat after me."

Clementer spent the next few minutes listening to both the children, reciting the words over and over again, until she was sure that they would never ever forget them.

"Now, you must return to your journey and I will bid you farewell. Goodbye, my special ones, be safe."

She turned her back to the children and they both knew that they must start walking again, nothing more could be said to Clementer. As she disappeared into her world, once again they started to walk, not knowing what was ahead, but both feeling safer, as Luke clung very tightly on to the blue triangle in the palm of his hand.

"When can we rest, Luke?" asked Sophie, "I am so hungry and tired."

"Soon, we must keep moving," Luke replied.

They were now walking on short grass which appeared to be quite wet on their trainers. They were leaving the tunnels and moving into an area quite different from before, there seemed to be more light and an open space ahead, which appeared to look like a large concrete playground. One swing was placed in the middle, but unlike the swings back home, it was different; four very large and heavy chains were attached to a very large settee, three large cushions were laying on the settee, and three for the seats. It was the best-looking settee that the children had ever seen and even better, it could swing. As Luke and Sophie were so tired, they could not wait to sit on it.

"Wait," Luke suddenly said, "This could be a trick."

Luke walked over to the swing, cautiously looking around, but no one appeared. They wanted some fun and somewhere to relax their tired feet and here it was, so they sat down together and started to swing. The settee was so comfortable and the movement of the swing nearly sent them both to sleep. As they looked up at the very large chains attached to the swing, they realised they were being watched, for sitting on top of the chains were a pair of tiny white doves.

"Well," said Sophie, "Look at them, Luke." Luke stared up at the two birds above, on top of the heavy chains. "Do you think that they are here to help us, Luke?" Sophie asked.

"I am not certain," Luke replied, "Let's ask them."

So he did, but the birds made no connection with the children. They just carried on sitting very quietly above them.

"I remember when the teacher, Miss Young, told us that two doves together is a sign of peace, maybe that is what they mean," Sophie said.

"I must say you are quite right; it is time to rest and be peaceful and this swing is here for you to do just that."

"What did you say just then?" Sophie asked Luke.

"It wasn't me," Luke replied, "It was them," pointing his finger up to the birds.

"But birds cannot talk," Sophie said.

"They can," replied Luke. They tried to make a conversation with the two white doves but they said no more. The children made themselves comfortable and in seconds they were both fast asleep on the settee swing.

"Good," whispered one of the doves, "They are resting. Now we must fly," and away they went, leaving Luke and Sophie sleeping peacefully.

When the children woke up, they noticed that the doves had gone and after having such a restful sleep, they both felt much better, although neither knew how long they had been asleep and above the ground, all the children's families had not even noticed the children's absence, as time there was standing still.

On waking, the children both knew that they must continue their journey so they headed off across the playground, both not knowing what was ahead or what direction to take. As usual, Sophie followed Luke; they now had the energy to walk much faster after their sleep. Luke noticed some large bushes up ahead and clutching the blue triangle in his hand, he headed for them with Sophie following closely behind. Both Luke and Sophie had noticed before they slept that the humming had stopped. Maybe the direction that they were taking was the wrong one. They were remembering what they had been told. The Tabots communicated by this sound, where it was strongest is where the Tabots would be found, so perhaps they needed to take a different route! Evil eyes were watching the children from behind the bushes. The eyes were on duty for the Tabots. A quick glance and you would guess that they were tennis balls but no, these were the evil eyes. There were ten eyes behind the bushes, they were darting to and fro, looking in every direction, and unfortunately, they had already spotted the children. Any eye contact with the children would be fatal. For Luke and Sophie to stay alive, they must avoid looking at the eyes, even for a very short time. Luke could see the bushes ahead moving and stopped Sophie from walking. She waited for his next move and it was then that Luke noticed the triangle in his hand vibrating gently. Did this mean danger ahead or just the opposite? Any change with the triangle must be noted. Luke remembered what Clementer had said earlier.

"You have one hour a day of power to help you and you must remember how to activate the triangle."

Luke said the powerful words in his head twice, so as not to forget them.

"Look," Sophie said. As she pointed her fingers upwards, the ten eyes were darting across the sky and to Luke and Sophie, they looked just like coloured tennis balls. They were going too fast for the children to catch, or even to focus on any one ball, but the eyes were clever and they needed to attract Luke and Sophie's attention.

"Shall we try and catch one?" asked Sophie, with excitement in her voice.

"They are going too fast," replied Luke.

The triangle vibrated more each time a ball passed Luke's head. If only it could speak, it would be telling the children how much danger they were in. The eyes started to slow down and the children watched them.

Up and down they flew, to the left and to the right, round and round and round. The children could not believe how quick they moved, each second they slowed down a little more, the children still followed their every move.

"Are they flying tennis balls, Luke?" asked Sophie.

"I can't see yet, Sophie, they need to slow down," replied Luke.

The more movement the eyes had, the more the children were focusing on them.

"Are they tennis balls?" was their question, or something else. The eyes were very clever, they knew the children's thoughts.

"Why don't they stop?" asked Sophie.

"Perhaps they want us to follow them," replied Luke.

"But in what direction? They have so many."

One of the eyes flew past Sophie at great speed so she decided to follow that one, rather than watch them all. It was flying towards the bushes, where they had first noticed it, it was so fast they had to run to catch it up, it was too hard to grab it with her hands, as it disappeared into the thick bushes. "There you are," Sophie said, parting the leaves with her hands. The eye had come to rest as she peered down into the leaves. Sophie was staring at the eye that she thought was a tennis ball, she began to feel her left eye starting to water, and then to itch, followed by her right eye. Wiping her eyes with her sleeve Sophie suddenly realised how blurred her vision felt, until with horror, she realised that there was no vision and her eyesight had completely gone. Darkness was all around her. She had no sight and she was very scared. She heard Luke calling her name but she could not see him.

"Sophie. Sophie, where are you? I can't see you, Sophie," Luke was shouting at the top of his voice.

It was then that Sophie realised Luke had lost his eyesight too. They were both blind.

"Where are you, Luke? Please find me, I can't see you."

"Me too," Luke replied.

He had remembered the triangle's power but he had dropped it on the ground and had spent the last few minutes trying to find it. Searching around on his hands and knees, Luke was getting very frustrated, his eyes were very sore and his hands were sore too. The stones on the ground felt sharp as he desperately searched for the triangle.

"What are we going to do, Luke?" cried Sophie.

"Stay calm, Sophie, I will find the triangle if it is the last thing I do."

The evil eyes had left; they knew that their mission had been done. The children could no longer see and their journey could no longer continue.

"Those were eyes, not tennis balls," Sophie shouted.

"I know, I saw them too," replied Luke.

A sharp stone cut Luke's thumb as he carried on searching for the triangle and a small drop of his blood fell to the ground.

"Damn, it's raining," said a little voice from the ground.

Luke had heard this remark.

"Whoever you are, please help us."

And then the voice said, "I can't stop, it's raining, I hate the rain."

Not knowing who he was talking to Luke, replied very bravely, "Please stop. Can you see a blue triangle anywhere?"

"A blue triangle? What shape or form would a blue triangle be?" replied the little voice from the ground.

Luke drew the triangle with his hand in the ground.

"Well," said the voice, "there is one of those lying there."

"Please show me where?" Luke cried.

Not knowing who he was talking to was very frustrating and scary. A few moments passed before the voice spoke again.

"Can you stop the rain, I hate the rain, don't you?"

Luke thought carefully before he answered.

"I can stop the rain but only if you give me the triangle."

"You can? That is brilliant, wait one moment."

Luke waited and waited with patience.

"Luke, what is happening, who are you talking to?"

"Don't worry," Luke replied. "Stay still and quiet, we do not want to frighten the little voice."

"Here is your triangle, now you must stop the rain."

Luke took his T-shirt off and wrapped it around both of his hands, not knowing which one of the two was bleeding.

"Good," he heard the voice say. "Now that the rain has stopped, I must go. I have so much to do."

The little voice had been a small creature of the underworld called a ratel. If these creatures ever got wet, they would disappear, so their fear was the rain and of course, any water, and luckily for Luke and Sophie, the ratel thought it was raining. Luke closed his eyes and started counting to five. Speaking out loud, he repeated the words "Light and love, send to me light and love, for all to see." Opening his eyes, to his amazement, he could once more see just as clearly if not better than before, and Sophie, of course, could see too. She ran over to Luke and gave him a big hug.

"I was so scared, Luke."

"So was I," Luke replied.

He looked down at his hands and then at the ground below but there was nothing on the ground and no evidence of the little voice, just a T-shirt covered with his blood, but the wound had stopped bleeding now, just like the rain had stopped.

Once more, they must continue their journey together, knowing now that they must trust no one, only each other. Even though they had both gained their eyesight back, their eyes were still feeling very sore but, to the children's relief, there was no sign of the evil eyes. So, on they went. The sky was beginning to get dark and they knew that they must move on and walk at a quicker pace before darkness fell once again.

"Listen, Sophie, can you hear something?" asked Luke. Sophie stopped walking and listened; she could hear it too. The humming had started once again and they knew that the Tabots were ahead.

"We have the triangle, so don't worry," Luke said calmly.

Sophie felt like turning around and walking back. She was very hungry and her thoughts were on the party she had been invited to. Anna always celebrated her birthday in style; there would have been a disco too, as well as lots of good food. If only she was there now, amongst her friends. If only Flueller would appear and take them back to the bottom of their garden. *If only*, she was thinking. The humming was getting louder with every step that the children took but Luke was not worried about it at all, he knew the power of the triangle which he held safely in his hands.

"Hello, Luke. Hello, Sophie," and to the children's surprise, they saw a familiar figure in front of them. Flueller was sitting a few yards ahead on top of the small boulder on the ground, both her wings were still on her shoulders and she was smiling at Luke and Sophie.

"You have done very well, children. I am proud of you both, but for now, it is time to rest, eat and be happy."

The children could not have heard anything better than these words; they were tired, they were hungry and they needed to laugh.

"Come, sit with me," Flueller said, and minutes later, they were both tucked into a feast consisting of leafy clover heads, which tasted delicious, and afterwards, cupcakes of all colours; the purple tasted the best, they all agreed. They drank from tulip heads filled with a cool syrup drink which tasted very sweet and was very filling. To finish the meal, there was a small square which tasted of chocolate, although Luke and Sophie doubted that it was. They were full to the brim. The rest of the time, they were laughing at the stories Flueller told, how once she was asked to dance in front of the primrose queen and she tripped and fell straight into the bluebell trifle, oh, and the time she drank too much nectar juice, resultantly falling down the well at farmer Till's farm. Nectar juice was always avoided by fairies as it was very strong. How silly she had felt and what a bad head she had suffered in the morning. It was good to laugh again with Flueller and so good to see her again. Flueller could not stay too long on this level with Luke and Sophie, which they sensed as Flueller started to become quite restless.

"You have to go now," said Luke.

"Yes, Luke, I do," replied Flueller, "I wish that I could take you to the Tabots and my family, but this is impossible,

I would die before I reach them. You, as humans, can tolerate the Tabots' energy whereas us fairies cannot. You do understand, don't you?"

"Of course," the children replied together.

"Then I must go, but I will promise to meet you both on this level on your return."

As Flueller left, Luke and Sophie felt a very strong need to fall asleep and seconds later, they did just that. Sophie had dreams that she was back home eating her favourite food. Luke had dreams that he was fighting the Tabots and saving many people from their evil energies. In his dream, the Tabots were just ugly little people with strange ways, but in reality, they were much worse. Sophie woke up first, hoping that Flueller would be back, but to her dismay, there was no sign of her. Luke then woke up and stretched and yawned.

"Well, that feels better," he cried.

They brushed themselves down and stood up. While they had been asleep, the sky had become quite dark again.

"I hope that we have seen the last of those evil eyes," Sophie cried.

"Me too," said Luke, "I hated not seeing, that was awful."

With their energy back, they started once again to follow a brick path before them, but this was not just any brick path.

"Hang on a minute," Sophie cried. As she looked down at the pathway before her, she realised that every second brick had a little face upon it, looking up at her. The faces were all totally different, not one face looked the same. Some smiled while others were looked sad and angry. Sophie then realised that the faces were also chatting with each other as though they were in conversation together.

"Listen, Luke, they are talking to each other."

"Don't tread so hard on me," she heard one brick saying.

"Look where you are going," said another.

Luke stopped walking and told Sophie to stop too.

"If they can talk to each other, there is a good chance they can talk to us," Luke said.

By stopping, Luke and Sophie were wondering if the bricks would be more willing to communicate, so, standing still, they quietly waited. Nothing happened so they waited a bit more but the bricks were not talking, just whispering quietly. Bravely, once again, Luke decided to make the first move.

"Excuse me," he said. He was taught at home to speak politely to others. "Can you help us? We need to find the Tabots."

"Are you mad?" said a gruff voice from the second brick on the pathway.

"I hope not," replied Luke, "We have to find Flueller's family, she is a fairy and our friend."

"We know of no fairy here," replied the second brick, "but we do know the Tabots, they often run across our pathway. We keep quiet while they cross, you see the bricks with no faces, they were destroyed by the Tabots. We never knew how evil the Tabots were. We shouted to them when they crossed over and then they crushed our faces, the ones with no faces were destroyed because of this. You should turn back before you find out their evil ways."

"Yes, yes, go, go back," the others cried.

Luke and Sophie looked at each other, they knew that time and time again they were being warned about these people but still, they ventured into the unknown. It was almost like the energy ahead was drawing them closer, even though they felt like they had to resist it time and time again.

"Well," said the second brick, who appeared to be the leader of the others, "are you going back home or are you the brave ones?"

"We are the brave ones," replied Luke, still clutching the blue triangle in his hands.

"I suppose you both think that the blue triangle will save you, but you must understand that nothing can once you reach the lowest level."

Sophie shivered. She felt scared and nervous. The brick pathway was making a lot of sense.

"I want to go home, Luke, maybe there will be others who can help Flueller."

"Others?" replied the bricks, "There are no others, you are our last hope."

Each of the bricks with faces were smiling up at the two children. Many, many smiles. They knew those smiles must stay and only they could do that.

"The triangle will help you but you must do the rest and always keep together. Don't look at the Tabots, they will try and take your energy. Make no eye contact with them, remember too that they have guards who can fly, but only a certain distance from their camps. When you reach them, you must remember that they live in large round holes deep within the ground. The Tabots on guard fly around the holes and above but they cannot go too far as their wings are not strong enough, unlike fairies, who can survive for many hours flying. The Tabots will not understand you, they cannot talk, but they communicate by humming, you may have heard this already. They smell very strongly, as they are very dirty creatures. They use their nose to drill into the earth and to hide in every small corner when prey is around them."

"So, do you still want to meet them now?" the second brick asked.

"Well, do you?" another brick said.

"Yes, do you, do you, do you?"

"Shut up, Payto," said the second brick, "you say far too much these days."

The noisy brick was quiet once again, so too were all the others as they waited for the children to answer.

Luke replied, "Do you know how far we have to go before we reach the Tabots?"

The bricks all answered Luke's question together but they were singing now, rather than talking and in harmony. "If you follow the brick path, even though we think you are daft, you will reach the next level, but be aware of the devil. He will greet you at the door and the number will be four, you must be on your way, we would like you to stay, but your job that must be done, can be done, but you must run, now," they all shouted together.

With that said, the children grabbed each other's hands and ran, so fast that you would have thought that a large brown bear was after them. The faces had all disappeared, so they did not mind running across each brick on the pathway in front of them and when they finally reached the end of the pathway, they each looked back, little faces were smiling up at them, again so glad and thankful that the children had decided to tread on them to continue their journey.

Luke held the blue triangle in front of him as they spotted the door up ahead with the number four placed upon it.

"Okay," said Luke, "we know the devil, whoever he is, will be behind the door."

Sophie cried, "Do we have to open the door, Luke? Is there no other entrance?"

"No," replied Luke, "The bricks must know what they are talking about. Don't worry, Sophie, the triangle will help us."

Luke was now standing in front of a very tall red door. They knocked very hard and before their eyes, they saw a large pointed finger with very long nails coming out of the middle of the door. It was pointing at Luke and Sophie, and a voice followed the finger.

"You dare to enter this level?"

"Yes," replied Luke.

The voice replied, "Never will I allow such a thing," and with that, all went quiet.

"Now, what shall we do?" Sophie cried.

"We knock again," Luke said, sounding very confident.

So, he did, even louder than before.

"You dare to knock again?" they heard the voice repeat while the finger was still pointing at them both.

Suddenly, before the children had time to move away, they felt a cold breeze around them. With every second, the air got colder and colder and a strong wind blew around them, catching their breath until they very nearly stopped breathing. The finger got longer and longer, twisting around the children's bodies until it got to the point where the children could hardly breathe. Their only hope now was to rely on the blue triangle once more. Luke remembered once again the words to activate the blue triangle's powers.

"Love and light send to me love and light for all to see."

After counting five, the finger disappeared through the tall red door and the strong wind stopped, allowing the children to breathe once more.

"That was close," Luke said while trying to get his breath back.

"Thank goodness we have the triangle," Sophie replied.

They then saw that the tall red door was opening and they could now walk through.

"Careful," said Luke.

Being very alert, they walked through into the next level of their journey.

Chapter Four
Meeting the Tabots

The door closed behind them with a loud bang. The two children looked around them to discover what they had found on this side of the door. A strong light was there and a strong smell. A humming sound could be heard and both of them knew now how close they were to the Tabots. Remembering what the bricks had told them, they slowly walked up to the humming sound up ahead.

"Why do they smell so much?" whispered Sophie.

Luke answered with, "perhaps they never wash."

"Like you, Luke," Sophie replied laughing, but trying to laugh extra quietly wasn't easy.

Up ahead, they could see something flying around in circles. It must be the Tabot guards, and below the holes, where the Tabots could be found, the guards must have flown many times in a circle as the children quietly watched. They could not identify what the guards looked like as they were flying too high and too fast. There must have been at least twelve guards. Around the large hole was a lot of thick bushes and undergrowth, so the children decided that this was an ideal place to hide for a while. Maybe the guards would go back into the camp to rest or eat or even better: to wash their dirty, smelly bodies. Sophie and Luke crept very quietly into the undergrowth to wait and while they waited, they took it in turns to rest and sleep. Maybe this would be their only chance for a while. But the guards never stopped flying. They seemed to have so much energy; if only they would all use one wing; it may slow them down just like it did Flueller before she gained it back again. As Sophie slept, Luke watched as he clung on very tightly to his good friend, the blue triangle. The strong light still seemed to be with them. Just as Luke nearly dozed off, six of the guards left the others, diving into the hole below. *Perhaps the rest will follow*, Luke was thinking.

Luke woke Sophie and told her to be ready to move when the opportunity was right. Seconds later, the six other guards followed the others into the hole the children knew that they both would have to move very quickly before they returned. Moving out of the undergrowth, they crept towards the entrance to the Tabots' home, finally reaching the top of the hole, they looked down, catching the first glimpse of the Tabots' home. Below them was a very deep hole and at the bottom, many clouds floated around. There was no sign of the guards, no steps to descend down or slides, no more tunnels to walk through. They would have to just fall or dive into the clouds, but did they have the guts to do this?

They both knew that discussing this would make no difference plus, time was running out, so closing their eyes, holding their hands together and clutching the triangle, they dived straight down into the clouds below, falling down at a very fast pace, down and down, until they thought they would never stop, but they finally did. They had fallen through a level of clouds just like when you go on your holiday, the aeroplane descends, one minute you are above the clouds and then the clouds are above you. As they landed, mud was below their feet, although, on looking again they, could clearly see that it was not mud, it was thick, brown slime, very sticky and very smelly.

"Yuck," Sophie cried, "what is this stuff?"

"Not sure," replied Luke.

The sticky gooey stuff was pulling their feet down very firmly into the ground below. There was no way Luke and Sophie could walk. They were well and truly stuck in one place. Sophie looked up and she could see to her horror what was dropping out of the clouds; twelve winged Tabots and as each one dropped to the ground, they made a circle around Luke and Sophie. They could be seen very clearly now, each Tabot having two pointed wings and a very pointy nose. Also, their ears were very pointy, their faces were long as were their bodies, they had no feet or arms but what the children noticed more than anything was their very sharp teeth sticking out of their ugly little faces. Their teeth looked very sharp and strong. They seemed to love the sticky slime below them, almost washing in it as they landed. They were humming together, some louder than others. Feeling very frightened now, more than ever before, more than when they met Boris, the spider or the other characters along the journey's path. For many days, they had learnt about these evil creatures and been warned. Face to face with them, stuck firmly in the sticky, smelly slime, their only hope was the triangle's power which was still firmly in Luke's hands or so he thought, but on looking again, Luke realised he had dropped the triangle, watching it slowly disappearing in the slime below.

"No!" he cried.

The Tabots reacted to Luke's cries as the humming became louder every second. Reaching down into the slime, Luke tried to pull out the triangle before it disappeared forever but he was not quick enough. The triangle was gone forever and so too was the power with it. The children looked at each other with sheer panic in their eyes, glancing at the Tabots and waiting for their next move.

"Don't make eye contact, Sophie," Luke cried, "Remember what we were told."

It proved to be very difficult, as for some unknown reason, they both felt drawn to look at those ugly creatures before them. There was nothing more they could do except wait for the Tabots to make their next move. The humming sound was now changing, which must mean that their conversation was changing too.

If only they could understand what the Tabots were saying. They waited and waited, but so too did the Tabots, never moving, just watching Luke and Sophie all the time. The Tabots looked very much the same. Some a little shorter than others but all just as evil to look at. A few were swinging on the black vines. Luke guessed that they could have been the younger ones, maybe their children. Remembering the film he had once seen of the Gremlins, the Tabots seemed similar but far scarier and maybe just as mischievous, if there was more they could play with here. After what seemed to be hours rather than minutes, the Tabots stopped falling from above and the humming finally stopped for the very first time since Luke and Sophie had entered the underworld and silence could be heard. The only other sound was the bubbling slime below their feet. Luke felt very angry about losing the triangle and the power that went with it. Their feet were stuck very tightly in the oozing sticky slime. As hard as they tried, they could not move their feet, the more they struggled, the deeper their feet sank. The air smelt foul, the Tabots loved living in a dirty, rotten environment. The heat helped the mud and slime to grow, keeping the Tabots happy. There seemed no life there.

Although, Luke could hear something else, almost like a human voice. Perhaps his hearing was playing games with him, as was his mind, but there it was, again, as he concentrated on the sound, he slowly began to realise that he could hear a voice and no way was it Sophie's. *Could there be another human person with them?* He was made to believe from Flueller and the others they had met so far on their journey that only Sophie and himself were here. Maybe there were others and the voice that Luke could hear was of someone else trapped there too. The voice sounded quite close. Luke knew that it would be too dangerous to speak or even to shout so he decided to keep quiet for the time. He took another look around him. Sophie was standing quite close to him. She too was stuck in the gooey slime.

"Don't worry, Sophie," Luke whispered quietly. "We can get out of here, don't struggle otherwise, you will sink deeper," he said, reassuringly.

Sophie knew that he was right, so she tried to keep still.

"Did you hear that voice?" Sophie asked Luke.

"I did hear it," Luke said out loud. "Let's not say too much for now," Luke replied.

Sophie had now confirmed that there was someone else with them other than the Tabots. Maybe someone else had met

Flueller and followed her down. Luke felt a little better now knowing there could be another person involved with all of this. Another person could mean more help with the Tabots and a better chance of getting out of this awful place and back to their family and friends. More and more Tabots were dropping down from the sky, the ugly, smelly creatures humming as they fell. Luke and Sophie were dripping with not only slime but sweat as well.

The heat remained hot and clammy, the Tabots' ideal temperature. They were standing in a large swamp surrounded by long, slimy black vines stretching up to the dark sky above.

Nothing else seemed to be growing there. No flowers, no trees, no sign of any wildlife or birds; the mud was bubbling around them almost like a large volcanic eruption just about to blow. The one thing that the children didn't feel was hunger, and the reason for that was the powerful energy feeding them as well as the Tabots.

"So what do we do now?" Sophie whispered.

"We stay still and we wait."

Luke knew he could be patient. On the surface of the ground, while he had been waiting for Flueller to appear, he was very patient.

"Have they hurt you?" they heard a voice. Both looking at the direction it was coming from. *Maybe this was a talking Tabot*, they both thought together. A little girl was staring over at them. She was about seven years old with long blonde hair in plaits.

"Have they hurt you?" they heard a voice say. Both looked in the direction of where the voice was coming from. It was a little girl speaking to them. The top half of her body was clean but from her waist down, the children could see the sticky mud around her waist.

Over time, the little girl had spent many days in the underworld and slowly, day by day, she had sunk lower and lower into the sticky, smelly mud. Luke could not help staring at the little blonde girl. She had a look about her which reminded him of someone he felt he already knew. Maybe later it would come to him who it was, and at the same time, Sophie was thinking just the same.

"Have they hurt you?" a voice said once again.

Luke felt it was now time to answer the little girl's question.

"No, we are not hurt and my friend is okay too, thank you very much."

The little girl smiled very sweetly at them both as she clasped her hands together.

"It is so nice to talk again to others," she said.

Luke felt it was time to ask the little girl more about herself, if she was willing to talk.

"Why are you here? Have you been here long? Do the Tabots talk? Can we get out of here?"

"Which question do you want answered first?" the little girl asked Luke.

"Sorry," replied Luke, "there are so many to answer."

It was then that Sophie interrupted by saying, "Tell us your name first. We need to know what to call you."

What a good idea, Luke thought to himself.

"My name is Flutterbye, and yours?" she asked Luke and Sophie.

"I'm Luke and this is my friend called Sophie."

"What a pretty name Sophie. Would you let me have your name and you can have mine if you want?"

How strange, Sophie thought, *No one has ever wanted my name before and what a strange name to swap with Flutterbye,* she thought.

"Why were you called Flutterbye?" she asked the little girl.

"It is too dangerous to tell you for now, but you will know later when it becomes safer."

The two children knew that they must respect Flutterbye's wishes.

"The answer to your question as to why I am here is the same reason as you: to reach the lowest energy and destroy the Tabots."

Luke thought about Flutterbye's answer before he spoke again.

"Are you saying, Flutterbye, that we have still not reached the lowest level even though the Tabots are above us?"

"Unfortunately not, Luke. These creatures are not the Tabots, they are only their guards and guardians. The Tabots are much uglier creatures."

"How can anything be uglier than those?" Luke replied while looking up at the sky above.

"As you already know, if we were on the lowest level, the Tabots would now be dead. That is the law of the lands," she sighed and she continued, "Now, the next question, 'how long have I been here?' Not long before your journey started and yes, the Tabots talk, but only the two, Stuttbart and Noose. Oh, and your last question, 'how do we get out of here?' We wait for any chance we have and there may not be too many."

Oh dear, thought the children, *that did not sound too promising.*

"At least we know some more with your help. Thank you," Luke said to Flutterbye.

Looking at the little blonde girl, Luke noticed that her eyes had closed and she was sleeping. The questions and answers had worn her out and Luke was hoping not too much.

"Sophie," Luke whispered, "She is asleep, I hope."

"What do you mean, I hope she must be, please don't say that she could be anything else."

They both quietly listened and to their relief, they could hear very gentle breathing coming from Flutterbye's direction. How relieved they both felt.

"Maybe we should try and sleep while we can," Sophie said.

"Well, at least the slimy mud and whatever it was, was warm and the Tabot guards are not bothering us" Luke replied.

So, they both agreed that the only thing left to do was to rest and that was what they all did. Sophie dreamt that she was in her bedroom at home while Luke's dream was about fighting the biggest dragon in the world. Flutterbye never dreamt about anything as when she slept, everything would shut down and sleep with her. It seemed a long time before the sleeping stopped and the waking started. All the children opened their eyes at the same time, being careful not to yawn or move too much to disturb the slime around them, as they had no intention of sinking any lower than necessary.

Chapter Five
Flutterbye

The sleep had done them a lot of favours. The children had not realised how tired they had become. Flutterbye was the first to speak.

"Are you both fully awake?" she asked the children, "We may have a visitor."

"A good one, we hope," replied Luke.

Flutterbye laughed at Luke's comment.

"All is not bad down here. Many are but there are the odd one or two who enjoy being kind to us strangers."

Luke and Sophie both felt quite relieved to hear this. The children were keeping as still as they could because of the sinking slime around the lower half of their bodies. They suddenly noticed the change in the current of the slime. It seemed to be moving much faster, almost as something was starting to stir the slime with a large wooden spoon. Flutterbye noticed it too but she was well aware of the reasons for it. Tuckertip would be paying them a visit very shortly. It was time to tell Luke and Sophie about his visit.

"Before major panic, we must be aware of Tuckertip," she said with a very relaxed look upon her pretty little face. "Tuckertip is a slime monster but good and kind. He keeps a low profile until he gets hungry."

The children's faces changed after that comment from Flutterbye.

"You mean, we may be his next dinner," Luke replied with an anxious look appearing on his face.

Flutterbye was very aware of what Luke and Sophie were thinking so she quickly replied to Luke's comments.

"Tuckertip only eats the Tabots' guards. He likes nothing better than using his long arms and he has many to catch the guards, he gets as much from the catch as he does from the eating when they are caught. He will have no interest in all of us here but we may have time to ask him a big favour to help us get out of this swamp."

"You mean, he may be able to get us out?" Sophie asked Flutterbye.

"I give you no promises, let's just wait and see."

The slime moved more now, creating more of the foul smell the children had become so accustomed to. Faster and faster, the slime moved, but so too were the children, sinking slowly into the slime below their feet. It became very scary. When and how long would this monster take to appear before them? Never before had the children wanted to meet a slime monster more, and if the sinking slime did not take their lives, the terrible smell would.

It got hard for the children to breathe and the intense heat made the whole situation a hundred times worse.

"Let's sing," Flutterbye suggested, "It may help Tuckertip to wake and realise how hungry he is and he really should not sleep so long anyway," she said.

"But what do we sing?" asked Sophie.

"What do you both know?" asked Flutterbye.

"I'm not singing any of that girlie stuff," said Luke.

"Let's not be too fussy about this, Luke. After all, we are discussing our lives here."

Sophie started singing very quickly after this comment from Flutterbye, she knew how right she was.

"I said, who do you think you are, some kind of superstar? You have got to swing it, shake it, move it, make it."

It was very hard for Sophie to keep still. This was a song she loved dancing to back at home in her bedroom.

"I knew it would be this one," Luke cried.

Flutterbye instantly recognised this song; she had heard it many times before in the garden of Sophie's parents. Sophie would be singing this in her bedroom and when the bedroom window was open on the hot summer days, Flutterbye would be quietly singing it too as she rested on her mushroom at the bottom of Sophie's garden. Sophie realised that Flutterbye was singing it too.

"Do you like them too?" asked Sophie to Flutterbye.

"Do I like who?" replied Flutterbye.

"The singers to this song."

Flutterbye had to answer this very carefully. With luck, Luke came to her rescue.

"The Spice Girls, why do we have to always sing this?"

"Just sing and shut up, Luke."

Enough said, so they sang.

"Who do you think you are over and over again?"

Flutterbye was so relieved that she did not have to answer any difficult questions that the two may have asked her about these so-called sponge girls or whoever they were called. It never took very long for Tuckertip to appear, maybe he was not too keen on the children's singing or maybe he had decided that he was getting hungry. Tuckertip was very aware of the sound of the children's voices as he very slowly started to swim to the surface of the slimy swamp. It seemed to take a lot longer than before as his last meal included an extra Tabot guard. Tuckertip was a very experienced creature. Not only could he live amongst the most dreadful conditions but he had other skills too. When he did not need to swim underwater, he could use his strong arms to walk along the bottom of the deep swamp. Breathing was also easy for him. On his body, he had many tiny holes which helped him breathe for many hours at a time while he lived underwater. As he had no sense of smell, the swamp remained to him a good place to live and of course, food was plentiful while the Tabots were still there. He sometimes felt very lonely without others around, but he was used to it now. The sound of singing was music to his ears, maybe today, as well as a meal, he could have a conversation too.

Such sweet gentle voices, he thought as he lifted his big slimy head out of the swamp.

"Oh my god" was Luke's reaction as Tuckertip lifted his head above the water.

"How scary is that?" he said.

Flutterbye was well aware of the children's feelings right then and she felt that she needed to encourage them both.

"Now, you two, there is no need to panic, Tuckertip has no interest in you whatsoever, in fact, humans make him quite sick."

With that said, once again, Luke and Sophie lost their fear. In fact, they were both feeling quite excited to meet a real slime monster again. Tuckertip lifted his head higher above the surface of the water. He was hoping to see at least three Tabot guards. He had spent a long time asleep and he needed to satisfy his massive hunger. Several of his arms appeared on the surface vines above. He could see two but he was rather disappointed about the third. The singing had stopped and he noticed a familiar face. In a very loud, deep voice, he shouted: "Why, Flutterbye, are you still here?"

Replying to Tuckertip's question, Flutterbye said, "I have no choice. This swamp is getting stickier by the second and my friends are now stuck here too."

There was silence for a few moments as Tuckertip replied. "Are your friends the same as you?"

Waiting for the answer patiently, Flutterbye replied with "They are of a different breed but they still remain our friends."

"That is good to hear," replied Tuckertip.

Luke was thinking how much he would like to ask Tuckertip about his life in the swamp. He decided to just start asking the questions in his head. Hoping that this monster would not be annoyed but Tuckertip seemed far more interested in Luke and Sophie's life. He wanted to know where they had come from and why were they there. After about five minutes of questioning, he finally paused for breath.

"Do you have swamps in your country?"

"Maybe bogs," replied Luke, "but the swamps are in other hot countries like Australia and America and Africa."

"So, where are these places?" asked Tuckertip with interest.

Sophie replied before Luke, "Nowhere near where we live. You have to take a plane and a boat and save a lot of money to get there," she said.

"What is a plane?" asked Tuckertip.

"You mean, you don't know?"

"But why should I?" replied Tuckertip.

"You must remember," said Flutterbye, "Tuckertip has lived in no other place than this. This is all he knows."

"So, do you know what a plane is?" Sophie asked Flutterbye.

If Flutterbye had answered Sophie's question, the children would then know who she really was and for now this still remained her secret.

"Too many questions for now, don't you agree, Tuckertip?"

He agreed by waving his long arms high above the surface of the swamp, nearly catching a Tabot guard as he did. Tuckertip was getting bored with all this chit chat; he was very hungry. Flutterbye could sense his feelings as she was a very sensitive being.

"Can you help us?" she asked Tuckertip.

"Don't you like it in my swamp?" Tuckertip replied loudly.

Being aware of his loud voice, Flutterbye knew that she must calm him down, they needed his help to get out of the swamp and back on dry ground.

"We love your swamp but we have a job to do or rather, these children do."

"What's a job?" asked Tuckertip.

Flutterbye knew that this conversation was going to take some time so she said, "Will you help us? You are so big and strong and kind and…"

Tuckertip stopped her there by saying "Yes, I will."

And so, it was decided that he would help them all. And this was the plan: Tuckertip would pull each one of them out of the swamp on three of his many arms. As he reached up, he would reach very close to where the Tabot guards were flying. This could prove to be very dangerous but by doing this, Tuckertip could then grab hold of a guard with his other arms and receive his supper at the same time. The guards would think he was giving them the children but this would just be what they wanted them to think. Once the guards had been reached, he would swing all of them down onto safe ground and away from the awful smelly swamp. It was dangerous, but Tuckertip knew that he could do it.

He commanded them all to get ready so he stretched out his long and sticky arms for them to climb upon. This proved to be very difficult as half of the swamp seemed to be wrapped around each of them. Luke went first as Tuckertip stretched out his arm and Luke let him wrap it around his body. Sophie was next in turn and then Flutterbye. A few moments later, they were all ready for the next part of the plan. With all his strength, Tuckertip lifted all three from the swamp. It was very easy to do as the Tabots always struggled, making it very difficult. But he always got the better of them every time.

They were all very frightened now and any mistakes and they knew their lives would be over, and they were now very close to meeting the Tabots' guards face to face. But also, they must remember not to make eye contact at the same time. Meanwhile, the Tabot guards were feeling very frustrated. They knew that there was no way that they could reach the humans without Tuckertip grabbing each one with his vacant arms. The three children knew that Tuckertip would protect and look after them. Although Sophie was feeling very nervous, she had just been swung in front of the evil smelly Tabot above her, noticing his long sharp dirty teeth as he tried to snap her as she passed. Poor Sophie's face, she looked so frightened and scared. Everything became a nightmare as time ticked on. Her parents had no idea that she was even missing as the time stood still above the ground. How many times had she thought about her bedroom and her mother telling her to clean her room and put everything in its right place?

Never again would she leave it all down to her to do. Never again would she snap back at her for telling her to be in on time. And get up on time for school. All Sophie wanted now was to be back at home with her parents and never to set eyes on those dreadful mushrooms again. *Perhaps Dad could mow them down after all,* she thought. Another Tabot flew past her, snapping its teeth on the way. Little Flutterbye looked the calmest of the three, she trusted Tuckertip to keep them safe from the Tabot guards. She knew how he worked and what he was thinking. A tasty meal would be there for him when it was all over and so the chapter of the journey would be coming to an end. Tuckertip swung the three across the swamp on to safe ground below, gently releasing them from his strong arms on to the edge of the swamp. Luke, then Sophie and then little Flutterbye. His strong, long arms then returned, as with all his force and energy, he swiped three Tabot guards and gobbled them down whole, belching and mumbling delicious as he swallowed them. As Sophie, Luke and Flutterbye felt their feet upon the soft bank around the swamp, they all sighed with relief. They were safe now and Tuckertip had received his reward.

"He will leave us now and rest under the swamp until he is hungry once more," Flutterbye said.

"Can we thank him?" asked Luke.

"There is no need," replied Flutterbye.

So the huge mud monster disappeared below into the dirty water. The only evidence of his visit being several bubbles appearing on the surface of the swamp and, of course, three Tabots short above.

Chapter Six
Flutterbye's Story

Luke was the first to speak.

"So, where to now?" he asked Flutterbye facing her.

"Well, Luke," she replied, "we need to get out of here. Once the Tabots realise they have lost three of their guards they are going to reinforce, it will be very dangerous to hang around any longer than we have to."

All Luke could see was the clouds above and the swamp in front of them. Where was the exit? Perhaps Flutterbye knew.

"We have to move fast, children, before the Tabots reinforce their guards. It's time to use some magic dust."

"Where did you get that from?" asked Sophie.

"Never mind that, Sophie, all in good time, I will explain," she said with extra authority in her voice. She gathered the children in a very tight circle holding their hands and touching each of their feet with her own. She sprinkled the magic dust above their heads, mumbling some magic words at the same time, which the children could not hear or understand.

"Now, hold tight to my hands and we will fly."

Each of their bodies slowly started to lift from the ground suddenly. Gaining speed, all three started to head towards the clouds above. The swamp became smaller and smaller below their feet. In seconds, they broke through the clouds above. Returning to the level they had left before; Sophie and Luke had many questions for Flutterbye. Why magic dust was one? Why did she not use it earlier? They knew that Flutterbye was a fairy. Especially her name, it did sound like a fairy's name, although Luke and Sophie had not thought of this earlier. Sophie's stomach started to rumble and groan.

"How hungry am I?" she shouted.

Luke replied with "We all are, Sophie," and then another rumble was heard.

"When can we eat? Are we going to eat? What can we eat?" she asked anxiously.

Flutterbye opened her hand and showed Sophie the rest of the dust. From a palm of fairy dust earlier to a few specks now.

"I am afraid, Sophie, we have little dust left. Now, if you choose, we can have a meal but we can also go back to the surface."

"What do you mean?" asked Luke.

"Just what I said," replied Flutterbye. Luke was thinking about it but first, he felt that he needed some answers to the questions earlier. "We want to know who you really are, Flutterbye, and how you got hold of the fairy dust?"

She replied with "Well, now is a good time as any to explain."

So, she sat down on the green grass below, which was very warm and still; they could hear the humming below the ground and she began her story.

"Yes, I am a fairy." Sophie and Luke exchanged glances. "But as we all know, a fairy cannot leave the first level but a human being can."

Interrupting, Luke said, "But how did you change from a fairy to one of us?"

"Please," said Flutterbye, "let me explain with no interruptions. You both know Flueller. She is my mother, the queen of the fairy world. In a conversation, I heard her tell others in the fairy world about the waterfall of changes. How if you walked through it you would change to whatever you so choose. All of my family have been taken from the Tabots, except for Flueller, into their world. I miss them and want them back and so does the queen, my mother, Flueller. So one day in the past, I walked through the waterfall and became what I am now, but as you discovered, I fell into the swamp and ended up stuck for many moons. For how long, I don't know. I have always held onto this little fairy dust in my hand. Left to rescue myself and return to my world. You both know the rest."

"We heard water on our journey, was that the waterfall you speak of now?" asked Luke.

"Yes," replied Flutterbye.

"So what do we do, Luke, go back or carry on?"

Luke went very quiet but not for long.

"For Flueller and Flutterbye's sake, we must carry on, but can you come with us? You can help us get there, wherever there is," finished Luke.

"What do you think, Sophie?" Luke asked.

"Hungry," replied Sophie.

She was always thinking about food and how hungry she was. *Maybe there would be a chance of some spare dust to feed them all*, she was thinking to herself.

"That can be arranged," replied Flutterbye, "But are you sure that you both want to carry on knowing how much danger you could face?"

"Yes," they both said together.

So, with the decision made, Flutterbye threw the last of the magic dust into the air, repeating the same words quietly as she did. And in seconds, there appeared three large oak leaves on the ground in front of each of them. A large acorn then appeared, the size of a cereal bowl. Inside the bowls, a green liquid appeared which smelt very sweet but was cold and sticky.

"You don't need to know the contents, just eat, this has all the energy you need for a few days of travelling. It tastes good and I know that you will want more once it has passed your lips. There are no spoons because we have run out of dust. Just tip the bowls to your lips and drink," said Flutterbye with glee and excitement.

The two children were so hungry and they wanted to believe everything that the fairy was saying, so they tipped the bowl up towards their lips and started drinking the liquid inside. The food was so filling they had to leave some.

Flutterbye tucked into her bowl, drinking every drop, but she was used to this way of eating. All three of them had really enjoyed their meal, even though they had no idea what it was.

"Well?" asked Flutterbye, putting down her bowl beside her.

They both replied together: "We loved it, whatever it was."

So, their meal was over and their decision was made. The journey must go on and the Tabots must be destroyed. Their need to sleep was very obvious now. Leaving the lower energy down below meant getting used to the new, and after such a huge and filling meal, it was time to rest. So once again, they settled themselves comfortably on the soft warm ground which looked similar to our grass but seemed much softer to lay on. Still, the humming could be heard. Still, the Tabots worked below the ground. Both Sophie and Luke closed their eyes almost identically. Forgetting the danger below and ahead. Even Flutterbye was too tired now to be on guard, she slowly started to fall asleep. In next to no time, they were all asleep with no one on the lookout. They were now in grave danger as Stuttbart and Noose, the two brothers from the Tookrnan Tribe, were watching their every move. Their gentle breathing indicated to the brothers that the three humans were asleep.

"Now is the time," Stuttbart said to his brother, "But we must be quick. Let's take the boy, girls are useless on their own."

The first chance they could get to grab Luke, they would. They were very aware of how deep all three were asleep. So, they waited and they waited, and chose their time carefully, and there it was, the two brothers tiptoed lightly over to Luke. The only giveaway was their smell. But even that was not enough to wake the three.

"Take him, but do it now," Stuttbart whispered.

Chapter Seven
Without Luke

Sophie was the first to wake, rubbing her eyes. Still, she was feeling very full from last night's meal. At the same time, Flutterbye opened her eyes, adjusting herself to the light. Sophie looked around and noticed straight away that Luke was not there.

She called, "Luke, where are you?"

Silence, so she called him again. Again, there was silence. Sophie knew that Luke loved playing games with her but something was telling her that this was no game. Flutterbye could see that Sophie was starting to panic.

Where was he? Sophie was thinking. Flutterbye knew just what had happened but now she would have to explain to Sophie. Dragging Luke across the ground, Stuttbart and Noose felt very proud that they had taken this human so easily. There had been no fight. Luke was still sleeping peacefully. The last meal had contained some magic ingredients to encourage the body to sleep for long spells at a time. The Tabots were very aware of this, knowing that Luke would not wake up through his ordeal. Noose was holding Luke's legs while Stubbart was holding his arms. They did find Luke to be a little heavier than they thought. Tabot guards were very strong but very tiny in size. Maybe if Luke had eaten an even heavier meal they would have had more of a problem. Still sleeping, they dragged him over to the edge of their world, ready to drop once again through the clouds below. There was nothing now that Flutterbye could do to save Luke. Now, she would have to explain to Sophie. But being a fairy, she would not panic, she would stay calm and explain to Sophie in a calm and relaxed way that only fairies knew. Maybe he had gone for a walk.

"Where is Luke?" she asked Flutterbye.

So, now it is time, thought Flutterbye.

"As fairies, Sophie, we never panic. We stay calm when in danger so you must too."

"What do you mean? Has something happened to Luke?" Sophie asked.

The fairy sounded very concerned. There was silence for a moment as Flutterbye was trying to pick her words carefully.

"Luke has been taken by the Tabots back to their camp below the clouds."

"No, he can't have!" Sophie cried, "They would have taken us all."

"No, Sophie, we are females. They need a male energy to continue their plans. We are no good to them but Luke is."

Sophie looked very confused with Flutterbye's remarks.

"But why is that?" she asked the fairy.

"Let's sit for a while and once more, I will explain the reasons." So, they both sat on the warm ground, but without Luke. This was very strange to Sophie. She had spent a lot of time with Luke. He had been her friend and her companion on their journey. Even above the ground, she had spent every day with him. At school and at home. In fact, she was missing him already and she was so scared of the danger he must be in. A huge tear fell from her eye onto her cheek and then to the ground below. Flutterbye understood Sophie's feelings. She was very sensitive towards sad people.

"We will find him and bring him back," she smiled warmly at Sophie and continued, "If he does as he is told, they will not harm him."

"And if he doesn't?" replied Sophie.

"As fairies, we think positive, never negative. In our world, this is the law of our land. When we send out positive energy and thoughts, they will come back to us and help us to sort all our problems out. If we think negative and send those thoughts out, then negative things will happen and everything will end up wrong again. So what must we do, Sophie?"

If only I could think like a fairy, Sophie thought. *If only I was a fairy. If only Luke was here now.*

"I know how much of a shock this must all be and how much you are missing your friend. Please don't be sad and believe in the positive as my family have for many moons."

Flutterbye produced a very soft tissue in her hand and she passed it over to Sophie.

"Here, my friend," she said.

Sophie knew that Flutterbye was making so much sense and that she could always be trusted. She felt that her earlier questions needed to be answered. Why did they want Luke and not her or the fairy? So once more, she asked the fairy to answer her questions and once more, Flutterbye started to explain.

Luke found himself deep below the ground. Looking around, he could only identify his surroundings as being a cave, with just a little light to see. The heat was back again but there was silence. Even though it was hot, he found that he could breathe okay. But he was feeling very hungry. He knew that there would be no food there and no chance of finding any. If he had not been so hungry, maybe, he would have kept quiet, but if there was anyone out there that could hear him, he thought it was better than starving to death.

Shouting at the top of his voice, "If you are out there, please get me some food." He paused and listened for a reply but there was no answer. He called again but still nothing.

No one could help him and he would never see Sophie, Flutterbye or the others again. Especially his family and friends. Why did he love adventures and danger so much? If he ever got back to the surface, he would never go on another adventure again or crave for danger as he had so many times before. He now knew how dangerous this was. What would his parents say if he ever saw them again? Let's hope, he was thinking, he would see them, and soon. As much as Luke had enjoyed some of this adventure, at other times, he had been petrified. Yes, he really wanted to beat those Tabots, but now he doubted that it would ever happen.

Luke viewed his surroundings once more. The walls of the cave were very moist and hot. Lots of roots were growing through the cave walls and across the ceilings above.

He could see no way out, no doors or windows. He was standing on gritty sand and still silence was wrapped around him. Meanwhile, on the level above Luke, Flutterbye had started to explain to Sophie where she believed Luke would be.

"There are two Tabot guards that would have done this, the only ones that can talk. They would have taken Luke down to the next level. Probably putting him in one of the many caves on his own with no food. They will start moving him around to different caves, testing him on many levels. How much Luke can take would be up to him but the Tabots would test him to the limit. We know that Luke is strong but we will never know how strong. He may beat the Tabots but on the other hand, they may beat him."

"So, what can we do?" asked Sophie.

"Nothing," replied Flutterbye, "It's down to Luke now."

There was no more to say, there was no entrance down onto Luke's level. Until the tests were complete, the Tabots had ensured this. In front of Luke, a part of the cave wall opened, allowing him to crawl through. He started crawling on his hands and feet into another cave very much the same as the one he had left a few moments ago. The Tabots were very clever creatures. Nothing too difficult for Luke to begin with, although his energy was low with such an empty stomach. His rewards would be a meal after the task had been passed. Luke noticed that hanging from the cave walls were three hooks all the same size.

Okay, Do I pull all three or just one? Here goes, he thought to himself. Pulling the first hook was a lot easier than he thought it would be. On the higher level, Flutterbye had made a decision; there was no point in them both waiting around. For now, it would be better to go back to the surface.

She very much needed to meet up with her mum again, Flueller. After going through the waterfall, she could go back to being a fairy. So, after explaining this to Sophie, they made their way back. Sophie really wanted to stay there so as not to miss Luke when he returned. Flutterbye had made so much sense, explaining to Sophie that they should move back to the surface.

"But what if the waterfall has gone?" Sophie said.

"It will be there."

And it was, but Sophie knew that this was a different route than the one before and far quicker than their journey had been. On reaching the waterfall, which seemed no time at all, Flutterbye gave a long sigh. She was anxious now to get her wings back full time. She had missed flying so much and being above the surface in the garden. She missed the flowers and her regular meals and most of all she missed her mum. As she skipped through the fountains of water and Sophie walked around, she could not believe what she saw. The water seemed to be changing from clear to misty and then to orange and into a vivid strong red. It was hard to see Flutterbye through the colour. Sophie could just make out her small shape. After about a minute, the colours started fading and the mist again returned. Finally, the water started to clear and Sophie looked harder into the water to see the first glimpse of the little fairy. She did not need to look for long as Flutterbye skipped out with a very happy face. She started to shake her wings.

She did look the same, Sophie thought.

The same pretty blonde hair and pretty face. The only difference was a pair of delicate wings on her back and the clothes she was wearing. A red, short dress which was frayed at the shoulders and hem, two delicate shoes were on her feet. The same colour red as was the dress. A little red hat was on her head which reminded Sophie of an acorn. She had seen fairies in her books at home looking so much like this, but never in a million years would she believe that she was now in the company of a real one. But the most beautiful part of Flutterbye was her wings. As Flutterbye shook the last few drops of water from them, "It feels so good to be back to normal, it's hard pretending to be a human. Look, Sophie, I can fly again."

Sophie watched the little fairy flap her wings and lift herself from the ground, clapping her hands as she went.

"Wait for me," shouted Sophie, afraid of being left on her own, "Remember I am still a human and can't fly."

"But you can, Sophie, hold on to me and wrap your arms around my waist. Take care not to hold on to my wings and away we go."

They took off at a great speed, which surprised Sophie.

"Close your eyes now, this journey remains a secret to many except my family."

And in no time at all, they were both descending back down into Flueller's bed of feathers until they came to rest. Sophie was so relieved to find that she was so near the surface of the ground once more but also sad because Luke was still missing.

"Right, first things first," Flutterbye said, "We need to rest and then go find my mother later. I bet she is on the surface collecting more teeth."

Sophie started laughing, it sounded so funny and so normal. Being away from the underworld below, she asked Flutterbye how far her mother would travel to collect the teeth.

"Miles," answered the fairy, "Until she gets tired."

"But how does she know whose lost their teeth?" said Sophie.

"We live with magic, that's how we know."

A good enough answer, thought Sophie.

"Time to rest, then eat, then explore your garden again"

Sophie looked serious again and she replied, "I don't want to go home yet. I need to go back with Luke."

Flutterbye understood what her human friend was feeling. Maybe when they had rested again and eaten, she may want to see her family again, with or without Luke. Now she had powers back again, she brushed her small tiny fingers over Sophie's eyebrows which instantly sent her to sleep. Flutterbye sank down too into the soft bed and closed her eyes. With no fear of any danger, they both settled down to the long sleep ahead. Flueller knew that above the ground, the routine must go on. She had great belief that the two children would make it back. Having no idea that her daughter would return too. It was getting dark in the garden. An owl could be heard. Darrius, the badger, and his mate, Digger, were out looking for food. Hard work these days. Not many humans were feeding them. There were two kinds: ones a short distance away from Sophie's garden, Mr and Mrs Dunk. They would start bringing out their supper early in the evening, breaking the bread up and scattering nuts out over the lawn. For many months now, Darrius and Digger, two best mates, had fed from this lawn. They knew that the humans were watching them but they still ate and went back night after night. They felt safe and very full when they left. Not many humans would do this for them now. No one liked the badger much these days except Mr and Mrs Dunk, of course. Stepit, the brown fox, was active tonight. His cubs were hungry and needed their supper. The rabbits were hungry too.

Flutterbye was the first to wake as she knew she would be. Humans slept much longer than fairies. She let Sophie sleep while she prepared a meal for them both and when Sophie opened her eyes, there it was, in front of her, laid out on a pretty yellow leaf shaped like a primrose. Sophie felt wonderful as she stretched and yawned.

"How long have we been sleeping?" she asked Flutterbye.

"Till first full moon," answered Flutterbye. Sophie did not understand the fairy.

"Is that many hours?"

"Too many," replied Flutterbye, "No more questions, eat."

Sophie did not need to be told twice; she was starving. She never even stopped to ask what it was. She just gobbled it down. The fairy loved preparing food and watching it being eaten. She always had been told that she was the best cook in the fairy ring.

"Okay, it's now time to taste some fresh air. Are you ready, Sophie?"

Sophie nodded as they started their climb up to the surface. And in no time, they entered the mushroom door.

"There you are, back. And how do you feel?"

The garden felt so good and fresh. So different to the underworld. It was all too much for Sophie to take. She started to cry. So much had happened in so little time. If only Luke was there too, but he was not and she must be strong without him. The fairy interrupted her thoughts.

"You have one wish now, so what will it be, apart from getting Luke back, of course. We have no such power of magic to do that."

Without thinking, Sophie knew just what to ask.

"I want to see my parents again not to go back yet but just to see them at home would be good."

Taking Sophie's hand, Flutterbye tiptoed through the garden until they both reached the house. Mr and Mrs Barker were talking in the sitting room. The television was on in the corner of the room.

"What time do we leave tomorrow?" Mrs Barker asked her husband. He replied to his wife with, "Ten would be good if we can get Sophie up."

How strange, thought Sophie, *they still think that I am upstairs in bed.* But of course, to them, she was. Sophie was so interested in their conversation she never realised how close she was to the flowerpot underneath the window, until she sent it crashing onto the ground. Immediately, Mr Barker left his chair and opened the patio doors. Flutterbye grabbed Sophie, pulling her into the bushes.

"What was that?" shouted Mrs Barker.

"Must have been something in the garden. It's knocked over a flowerpot."

"Has it broken?" replied Mrs Barker.

"Yep, but don't worry, your pansies are still standing."

With that said, he left the garden and went inside. Sophie nodded as they left the garden and went back down the slope to the fairies' home.

Luke released the hook and then he waited for something, anything, to happen, but nothing did. Until finally, after several minutes, a small window materialised in the cave wall and a face appeared. The first glimpse of a Tabot guard for Luke. Luke felt a little faint. He had not eaten for a very long time now and maybe he would never eat again. Probably, he would starve to death in this horrible cave with this horrible looking face peering down on him.

Yuck, thought Luke, *Have I ever seen anything uglier than that, and it speaks.* Noose, one of the only two Tabot guards that could speak, started addressing him.

"So, Luke, what do you think of your new home?"

He has a strange voice, thought Luke.

It sounded almost like it was shaking. Almost like when someone is being horrible at school to you and your voice goes all shaky which means that you are scared. *But with this face in the window, I shall have to be brave, very brave now*, Luke thought. *Maybe the face will then disappear very much as fairies did in the garden when they were scared.* Bravely, even though Luke was not feeling this way, Luke answered.

"I am not scared of you."

"Never said you were, Luke," Noose replied.

Luke decided he would have to carry this through. He needed to know who it was and if it could help him. As the seconds passed, Luke saw the face was becoming clearer, so perhaps he thought it was not all down to hunger. The first question was: "Will another face appear if I pull all three of the handles on the cave wall?"

"Try it and see," the face answered.

Luke did not want to do it; one ugly face was enough for him, let alone three. And maybe they would not be as friendly as the first.

"I should be brave."

The face that now looked stern repeated, "You should be brave."

Here goes, thought Luke.

"Who are you? Why are you in the wall and how do I get out of here?" he said with confidence and a lot of strength.

"Tut, tut," Noose replied and he vanished in a puff of smoke.

Luke gained his composure, although he was very surprised. Such a short conversation with nothing gained. Although if Luke had thought about it, he had been very strong and brave once again. So, there was nothing for it except to try the second hook in the cave wall. He pulled the hook and waited, just like the first time, and once more, the second face appeared. This time, a similar face as the first, but this face looked scarier and, you guessed, well done, this was the second Tabot guard called Stuttbart. He could also talk. They looked so alike; they could have been the same face. The only difference was Stuttbart had more sharp teeth hanging out of his mouth than Noose.

"You going to disappear as well?" said Luke bravely to the face in the cave wall. Unlike the other Tabot guards, you could look at these in the eyes. If not, no doubt, Luke would be dead already. Luke was not aware yet that these faces were Tabot guards.

"I just may or may not," replied Stuttbart.

With the same voice as Noose; the reason for that was the Tabots had only one voice box so they all sounded the same.

"But if you pull the third hook," Stuttbart added, "you may see a face which could help you or it may be the biggest mistake of your life."

Stuttbart laughed in a very loud and aggressive way. So, Luke had a choice and he must now decide what to do. He so wanted to get out of the cave and eat some food. Maybe the hook would reveal the third face with a plate of food if he was lucky or he could be facing danger or even death. Before he could even ask for advice from the second face, it disappeared too. Luke felt so alone and unhappy. He remembered what his parents had always taught him. *Never rush in and make the wrong decision. Take your time and really listen to what you want.* Apparently, Luke's father had made a lot of money by doing just that. So Luke decided he had no other choice than to wait and think about this situation for a while more. Back on the surface, all was quiet in the garden as the early morning sun began to rise.

"Don't concern yourself, Sophie," Flutterbye said, "Luke is sensible and you know that. I feel he will be okay down there."

She sighed once more. How sad Sophie looked after seeing her parents and house once more, and missed her best friend Luke so much after their long, hard journey. She had every right to feel this way. *Let's think,* she thought as she bowed her head. *How can I change the way she feels?*

A thought flashed through her mind and then another and another, quick flashes of ideas and inspirations. Fairies were good at many things, especially that. She started to plan and make her arrangements to make Sophie happy again and as Sophie lay asleep; she lifted her wings and fluttered up to the surface. Knowing that Sophie would be quite safe in her safe house under the mushroom, she reached the door and pushed it open. The garden was getting warm and sunny. It was too wet for now for Flutterbye to take her little red shoes off, which she loved to do. It always gave the fairies lots of energy to run barefoot on the grass. If only all humans were aware of this, although a few were. Leaving her red shoes on, she tiptoed away from the safety of the mushrooms. Luke still debated in his mind as to what to do. He knew that he could not wait forever in the dark and smelly cave. Hungry and unhappy, there was no time like the present. He now felt very sure what he must do. He reached up to press the last of the three hooks on the cave walls. He could hear the humming from the cave wall which he guessed to be the Tabots. The humming got louder and louder until Luke could not stand the level of humming. The walls changed into many faces. No space was spared from each evil little face. Much uglier than the last. Until all the walls had gone to reveal the faces and Luke could only guess that these were Tabots. Not the guards, but the real ones, and they looked much eviller than the guards. Luckily for Luke, their eyes were closed but their mouths were open and the humming became too much for Luke's hearing, who shut his eyes in case they opened theirs.

Please stop, he thought but the humming never did. He could only wait and let fate take its course. He tried to concentrate his mind on something else. Just to block out the awful noise, but it didn't work. After a time, the humming stopped. This was the Tabot's next trick. By doing this, they thought that Luke would open his eyes, thinking the faces had gone away. Luke was a clever boy and he knew how much trickery there could be down there. The poor Tabots were impatient creatures. Never wanting to wait for nothing, so, they disappeared just as Luke opened his eyes. Luke was so relieved that the humming had stopped and to see that the faces had gone. He had learnt the art of patience, a very important lesson.

Chapter Eight
The Reunion

Flueller had collected many, many teeth this time in her acorn basket. It had been a very eventful journey. It was now time to go back below the surface and count how many she had collected through the night. There could have been one more from a little girl called Tracy but it was not quite ready, just loose. Perhaps tonight, when she went out again, she would find it under her pillow. *Yes*, she thought, *she would come back later to collect it*. Toreller, the fairy necklace-maker, would be so pleased with her collection of teeth inside the little bag made of leaves and twine. She was so tired she could not even raise her wings for the last part of the journey to her home below the third mushroom. So, being very tired, she slipped down the root into her bed below. Straight on top of Sophie, sleeping, although Flueller was very tiny, she still startled Sophie. Disturbing her enough to wake her up. Flueller looked below her, she knew her bed of feathers felt to her like the greatest in the world, but she was shocked that if felt so uncomfortable. What on earth would have caused it? All sorts of things went through her little mind. As did Sophie's. At the same moment, their eyes met and a large smile appeared on both their faces. The reunion had begun and two very good friends had once again met. Sophie was so anxious to tell Flueller about Flutterbye. She knew what a special moment this would be. And so, she began to discuss her. Their story never stopped for breath until all had been said.

"So, where is my dear daughter?" asked Flueller.

"While I was sleeping, she left. I guess for more food and to find you, Flueller," replied Sophie.

"Then we must find her."

Flutterbye was feeling tired too. Arrangements were being made for a party in the garden. A good place for this would be behind the mushrooms. The grass was longer there, no chance of being seen and the small folk would be happier playing in the long blades of grass. Especially her dear friend, the field mouse. They loved playing amongst the blades and weeds. The babies must have been born by now. Even more reason to celebrate. How exciting for them and all the others who loved this garden so much. She needed to get hold of

Dizzy, the father of the field mouse. He was a very clever mouse and would have some good ideas. But that must be later when the sun went down. For now, she would look for the team of cabbage butterflies. *A little tricky*, she thought, as two moons ago she had remembered a confrontation with a group of butterflies as they all looked the same and had no names. Flutterbye did not fancy speaking to them again. Harsh words were said by all. But she knew that if they were not included in the activities, they may ruin everything. Most of the butterflies felt that the garden was theirs and no one else's. Flutterbye remembered the argument very well. It was a hot afternoon and all the butterflies were out enjoying the sunshine. Flutterbye's mother Flueller had sent her out on an errand to gather leaves together as she was running out of her little bags to carry the children's teeth in. Flutterbye was resting underneath the cabbage leaves. The day was very hot and sticky. The largest of the butterflies demanded that Flueller leave and find another place in the garden to rest. Flutterbye was not used to being spoken to in such a rude manner. An argument developed and every cabbage butterfly insight, which were many, joined in. Poor Flutterbye had no backup, her family were attending to matters below the ground.

This was before the Tabots came and took them all away. The large butterfly had lashed out at the tiny fairy, damaging her wing which took several moons to mend. Flueller told her daughter many a time after never to talk to the group of butterflies again, but Flutterbye knew that she would need their help in setting up the party so, with no hesitation, she crept on hands and knees over the largest cabbage leaves at the bottom of the garden. Hiding her body and wings from view as the team of butterflies came and went, minding their own business and enjoying the sunshine; she would have to pick her moment carefully, trying to listen to their mood as she hid under the leaves.

"Where's that stupid friend of yours?" asked the first butterfly.

The second butterfly replied, "I guess with that stupid friend of yours."

They both laughed out loud. *Yes,* thought Flutterbye, *it sounds as if they are in a very good mood today.* Bravely, she appeared above the cabbage leaves. The first butterfly instantly recognised her.

As he moved closer, "Want your wings damaged again? Not just one this time but two."

There was silence in the garden as Flutterbye thought of how to reply. A very clever thought came into her mind.

"Yes," she answered. "My wings have been mended by the strongest moon in the night sky but the strongest has the most power, a secret power, which if tampered with, will ignite and be as strong as all the full moons put together."

As she stopped, she noticed the expression changing on the butterflies' face. They looked scared and very nervous. They all knew how powerful the moon could be. But all the moons put together could wipe them out with one magic word from this very brave and stupid fairy. By the butterflies' expression, Flutterbye knew that she had won them over and now she could start telling them about the plans for the party.

"If you don't help me to arrange a party for my friend, I will use all my power on all of you."

"We can help you, what do you want us to do?"

Flutterbye looked at them all as she continued.

"Get all the mice together, all of the butterflies and anyone else that you can. We are having a party. You can come if you behave."

Well, the butterflies loved a good party so they agreed to do it for Flutterbye. As they flew away together, *how easy was that,* thought Flutterbye, as she smiled to herself. Maybe she had told a small, white lie but in this case, she had no choice. Her life had been put at stake. Therefore, it was the only time lying was allowed in their lifetime and in the human lifetime. It was time to go back to her friend below the ground. If Sophie was awake, finding herself alone would be very unfair after what Sophie had just been through. With the arrangements beginning to happen, she flew back down to her home. Down the chute to safety and sleep. Flutterbye had no idea who would be greeting her there. In next to no time, she had arrived back, a little doorway led from her bed into a large storeroom full of teeth of every shape and size. They had all been numbered and sized into compartments in the side of the four walls. On the floor still, teeth to be sorted tucked away in bags. No sign of Sophie there. So, Flutterbye went through to the next door into the next room. And it was there that she was greeted by Sophie and her mother Flueller. No words could be said, only hugs and cuddles. No crying, just very happy faces and a very happy human, Sophie. There was so much to catch up on as there always was. So much to tell and explain and Flueller was a very proud mother as she realised what her daughter had been through for her family.

No words would describe this very special moment as they all three hugged over and over again. When they finally stopped hugging, Sophie said, "I wish Luke could have been here with us."

"We wish that too," Flueller cried, "Luke has to convince the Tabots that he is stronger than them. He has to show strength and determination. We know he can do this and I am sure you know this too, Sophie."

Sophie remembered how strong he had been at school how he had stuck up for her every time, never failing to be there for her always. But that was at school, never as scary and dangerous as that.

"Remember," Flueller said to Sophie, "be positive always and good will happen."

"But I miss him so much," Sophie started to cry out loud and it seemed to last for ages.

Flueller had a very worried look on her face. What if Sophie never stopped crying? Their home would flood and that could be very dangerous for them all. Human tears were very large, almost like a large puddle when they rested on the ground. She must stop the crying as soon as she could. Sternly, she repeated to Sophie.

"Be positive and all will be well."

Flutterbye thought now was as good a time as any to tell them both about the party. Maybe this would be the answer to Sophie crying, and it worked, as we know that Sophie loved a good party. The party arrangements were being discussed together in the garden. The team of cabbage butterflies had already spoken to ten frogs sunbathing around the little pond in the garden. They all agreed on how exciting it would be. Then they talked to the field mouse and the dormouse.

"As long as they behave," Dizzy, the field mouse, stated when the butterflies told him about the party. He had also had a bad experience at the last garden party, but he would rather not talk about it, thank you.

"Will the hedgehogs come? And the badger family?" asked Dizzy.

"One never knows," replied the butterflies together. They always seemed to stick together these days, especially when they were discussing a party.

"What about food?" Dizzy asked the largest of the butterflies, who always spoke the loudest. Dizzy said, "I suppose we have to bring our own but it's in short supply, we have a problem feeding our family of hedgehogs."

"Well, remember, everyone, this is the first time a party has been held for ages in this garden. Let's have a good time, what do you all think?" said Dizzy.

He stopped talking and waited for an answer. Now, all the garden folk and the fairies and the insects and birds loved a party. The garden was filled with excitement as all involved were discussing the party well into the night. In fact, the hedgehogs had forgotten to feed their babies due to the excitement going on. Back under the ground still, Sophie and Flutterbye were discussing the past situations while stopping for hugs every so often when they were needed. Luke was so relieved that the humming had stopped and the Tabots had gone. He now had to get out of the cave but there were no more hooks to pull and no doors or windows to open. Luke then noticed a large crack appearing on the floor of the cave. The crack got wider and wider until Luke realised that the whole of the cave floor was opening and there was no way he could stop himself from falling through and down he went, falling at a very fast pace into the darkness below, falling and falling, deeper and deeper into the ground below the cave floor, until he finally stopped and his feet felt the weight of the ground. It felt rather soft under his shoes, he must have been falling for a very long time. He was standing when he finally landed, balanced on his feet. Luke felt quite sick, there had been no food in his stomach for days and he was very worried that soon he may starve to death. He must search around for some food now that he was out of the cave. Looking around, he guessed he was in a long corridor. It was easy to see as it was light. He could spin around in a circle so there was a lot of room to move about. He must follow the corridor until he reached the end. Luke started to walk, the corridor twisted and turned but nothing changed except the curves in front of him. On and on he walked, never stopping, trying all the time to forget how hungry he was. The only sound he could hear was his stomach grumbling.

"No food, no food."

On and on he went. *There must be an end soon*, he thought. Standing just up ahead, he realised, there was a figure, tall and straight. He would go on now and see what or who it was. Finally, he reached the figure. It was a statue made of black metal. It held a large straight stick in its hand. The size of the statue itself. It could have been mistaken for a tall human being. *Maybe it was, once upon a time,* Luke thought. The statue took up all of the corridor and the only way for Luke to pass it was through the statute's legs to the other side, and it was there he found another entrance. An opening with no door. Just a small archway to climb through, so, bending down a little more, he went through and it was there that he met the Tabots once again. He knew because the humming had started and the heat had risen very high. His immediate thought was to close his eyes from the Tabots.

He had no need to because the Tabots had left their eyes above, they no longer needed them on this level. There were hundreds of Tabots. They were all busy working. Luckily for Luke, they had no idea he was there. With no eyes to see him.

Luke still knew how careful he would have to be. If the Tabots felt that he was there, they would kill him instantly, so Luke hid behind a large crate and watched carefully. They seemed to be lifting machinery out from those crates and knocking something together. The machinery looked very heavy for their little bodies. Many of the Tabots helped to lift together as they carried on humming at the same time. It was still very smelly there.

Luke knew now that the Tabots were very dirty and smelly creatures. For a long time, they worked while Luke watched. Luke could not understand what they were building.

Suddenly, Luke's stomach started to roll around and make a loud rumble and the Tabots heard it too, they all stopped working and sensed Luke's presence hiding behind a crate. They felt Luke as he gathered speed and ran very fast towards the opening he had come through earlier. As he bent down to go through, two of the Tabots grabbed his legs and pulled him back. Several others pinned him to the ground as they tied his arms and legs to the ground with some sort of thick rope. Luke looked up and he could see all the Tabots looking down on him. Their ugly little faces and long sharp teeth pointing down onto his face and their smelly bodies dripping sweat onto Luke's body. Luke knew that they could not see him, only sense where he was and feel their way around to tie him to the ground. He thought that his life was over now and that he was going to die but that's not what the Tabots wanted. They needed to understand humans and how they worked. They had no intention of killing Luke.

After a few moments, they started their work again, leaving him there. It seemed like many hours to Luke before they stopped. A loud whistle blew, as soon as this was blown, the knocking and banging stopped and all of the machinery was put down. Then they gathered together with their heads bowed down and started chatting together in the way that they communicated, by the continued humming. The rope was very tight on Luke's arms and legs. The more he struggled, the tighter the rope became. Luke looked up and noticed a little spider hanging from a small web barely inches from his face. From this spider, another one appeared as the web became filled with little black spiders. Luke was petrified as he had no way of moving anywhere and slowly a spider started to fall onto Luke's body, and slowly, more and more until Luke's body was covered in small black spiders and there was nothing Luke could do; he shut his eyes and screamed and screamed very loudly.

"Are we scared, Luke?" Noose said, as he suddenly appeared among the other Tabots.

"Do you fear the spiders?" Stuttbart continued, also appearing.

"Just undo me please and I will do anything that you say," Luke cried.

"Anything?" asked Noose.

"Yes," replied Luke.

"Anything?" asked Stuttbart.

"Yes," Luke said again.

"Biffay!" Noose and Stuttbart shouted together. One by one. the spiders climbed the web. It seemed to be ages by the time they climbed and Luke was free from them again.

"We want you to take us to Flueller, the queen of the fairies," Noose said to Luke.

"I can't," Luke said, "I don't know the way back."

"We do," they both chimed, "But we have to do this without the others knowing, do you understand? We know that you are hungry so we will feed you now and then take you back with us to the fairy queen."

Luke nodded, he must do as they say. It may be the only chance of getting out of there. They untied him and sat him up.

"Wait here," they said, "Noose will stay with you, I will get you food."

Stuttbart disappeared while Noose sat down by Luke. No one spoke. Luke was too weak and tired now to do anything. It seemed ages for Stuttbart to appear and when he did, Luke was barely able to lift his arms as he felt so weak. Stuttbart knew this as he put the bowl of food down in front of Luke.

"Eat," he said.

Luke slowly lifted the spoon out of the bowl. He did not really care less. Whatever the food was in the bowl set before him, he would eat it. Inside the bowl was some brown liquid that was runny with bits of green stuff floating on the top. He raised the full spoon to his mouth and swallowed the liquid inside without even thinking about the taste. He was beginning to fill his stomach and become strong again. When all the liquid had gone, he wiped his mouth with the back of his hand and realised how slimy his hand had become.

"Oh, go on, Luke, ask what it was. You know you want to know," Noose said.

"He is scared," said Stuttbart, "We shall tell you anyway, it was swamp water and the bits were seeds that grow in the water. Was it nice, filling, was it?"

Luke retched as he swallowed the last of the liquid down. *At least he was not dead,* he thought.

"Why do you want Flueller?" he bravely asked the two Tabot guards.

"She has all the answers," Noose replied.

"Answers to what?" asked Luke with an interesting look on his face.

"Never you mind, Luke, just you take us to her."

"But you can't leave the underworld," Luke said.

"Yes, but you can," they both said together.

Luke thought for a moment that if he could be shown how to get back to the surface, he would get home. Surely, giving Flueller to the Tabots would be okay. She would be with the rest of her family. They could all be together once more. He would see Sophie again and his family and friends. He could go home and leave that place forever. But on the other hand, could he do this to Flueller? His friend, risking her danger? He had another choice to make and soon. But he knew without even thinking what he must do, so he told the Tabot guards as they nodded their heads. And while the other Tabot guards were in deep conversation, together, they crawled through the arch into the corridor on the other side. They walked for a long way before they stopped and Luke looked up to the spot where he had fallen. Noose then explained to Luke that he must climb on their back and then they could fly back up the way Luke had fallen earlier. Luke obeyed their commands and together they left that level and ascended upwards, never stopping until, with some magical ingredient, they reached the level below the ground where the fairies lived.

Chapter Nine
Party Time

The party day had arrived and everything was being prepared above the ground. All the guests waited for their hosts. Flueller and Flutterbye and Sophie. They had never been so close to a human before and certainly never been to a party with one. Flueller had assured them all that it would be safe. Sophie was very excited and as all three opened the mushroom door and walked outside, all the garden folk cheered and clapped. What a welcome for them all. It was a lovely sunny evening as they all gathered together in the long grass at the bottom of the garden. Flueller had chosen a day when she knew that Mr and Mrs Barker were out for the evening. She had heard them talking a few days ago while they were busy gardening. Sophie was introduced to each and every one of them. *How friendly they all were. Except maybe the butterfly family, but they did try,* she was thinking. They all ate and they danced and they sang right into the night and early hours of the morning until it was time to rest and be still once more. As the last of the garden folk left, Sophie, Flueller and Flutterbye left too. Back below the ground, all had a special smile on their faces, especially Sophie. So the party had been a great success. Everyone was very tired as they all settled down to rest. Laying comfortably in their bed of feathers, Flueller heard it first. The humming and the smell which she knew so well. There were Tabots very close. She knew the signs. She did not want to panic the others yet so, she left her home and ventured below, through the hole under her feather bed, closing it as she left. Luke, Stuttbart and Noose were already there waiting for her. She saw them straight away. Fairies had no problem with their vision. She had met Noose and Stuttbart before and she was not scared of them.

"What do you want?" she asked the two Tabots, "Have you brought back my friend?" noticing Luke with them.

"Yes, we give you Luke, but we take you in exchange."

"I thought so," Flueller said. "You never give anything away for nothing."

Noose replied, "You know us well."

"So, what's it to be?" Flueller knew without thinking. "Hello, Luke, welcome back."

She walked towards the Tabots and gave Luke a big hug and a warm smile. Luke was so happy to see her but so sad that it had to be in such circumstances.

"Don't be sad," Flueller said to Luke, pushing him away from Noose and Stuttbart. "Go, Luke, go home," she cried.

Luke looked at Flueller.

"No, I can't leave you, Flueller."

"You must, my friend," she replied.

Noose and Stuttbart were becoming very impatient. They wanted to go back down to the underworld and show off Flueller to the rest of the Tabots. Flueller repeated to Luke that he must go but Luke still stood in the same place. Not wanting to let Flueller go. The exchange would have to be made. The Tabots became even more impatient. Luke could just not bear to leave his friend.

"Go now," she repeated, "Be brave. Sophie is waiting for you."

Luke knew that he must go now and he also knew that he would be back to find Flueller and bring her back. He hugged Flueller as the Tabots turned behind her, following her as they made their way back into the underworld. Luke opened the door and stepped into the bed of feathers, noticing Flutterbye and Sophie fast asleep. They were so tired from dancing all night. They never woke as Luke lay down with them. He would talk to them both when they woke. Noose and Stuttbart followed Flueller, on the same journey they had taken with the rest of her family, to their underworld below the ground.

Chapter Ten
The Second Reunion

As they all woke at the same time, the second reunion took place. Sophie was so happy to see her friend again safe and well. But very much skinnier than before. Flutterbye prepared them all some food as they were all so hungry once again. As they listened to Luke's story and the very sad news about Flueller, it was Flutterbye's time to feel sad but fairies didn't cry, they just went quiet for a while and then they became positive and strong.

"Right," said Flutterbye when she began to come out of her silence, "It's time to make plans of action and to get my family back."

"But how are we going to fight an army of Tabots?" asked Sophie.

Flutterbye answered, "Well, we use the teeth we have collected and stored, I knew they would come in useful."

She said with a smile on her pretty little face.

"Teeth won't fight an army of Tabots, they have evil teeth and they can bite," Sophie said to Flutterbye.

"Yes, I know, be patient and I will explain."

The next job after they had eaten was to collect all of the teeth that they could carry and start their journey down to the lowest level.

"What about Flueller, will she die before she gets down to the lowest level?" Luke asked. With great concern in his voice. He knew that the lowest level was not reached by fairies unless they changed into humans through the waterfall first.

"It changes if the Tabots take a fairy with them. If you venture on your own, then yes, you have no chance. She will be okay and if we follow them soon, she may have a chance."

So they picked up the bags of teeth, all that they could carry and headed off to rescue their dear friend and mother. Luckily, for Flueller, the two Tabot guards, Noose and Stuttbart, kept stopping to chat and to discuss their success in bringing back the queen of the fairies. How excited they were, they would become so famous when they reached the commander of their race and they would never ever be forgotten for bringing Flueller to them. Resting again, they talked amongst themselves. They had only reached the third level and they had a long way to go. Flueller knew in her heart that the others would follow her. They loved her too much to leave her down there. How lucky she was to still be alive and well.

Heaving the teeth on their backs, their journey started once again. As they left the safety of the home, stepping once more into the next level. Much had been controlled so far but much had been achieved too. Flutterbye had to have faith that her mother was still alive and well. The two Tabots were very quiet for a change. As they continued their journey, Luke, Flutterbye and Sophie found it very hard to carry so many bags of teeth, especially the little fairy. If they dragged them, the chances of the bags splitting and losing the contents were high. Luke was the one carrying the most. Being the strongest of them all, three bags were slung over his shoulders, whilst Sophie carried two bags over each arm and Flutterbye carried one with both her little hands in front of her. Being so hot in the underworld, it proved to be more and more difficult as their energy started to drain from them. Luke knew that the journey would be far easier as Flutterbye took the shortest route she knew. All their hold-ups and danger were on the other levels which Luke and Sophie had already encountered. Their biggest danger was yet to come. By avoiding the other routes, they would be walking into a very dangerous situation a little way ahead. To be fair, as little fairies always were, she would alert her two friends telling them the bad news.

"Up ahead," she cried, "we face danger, there is no way to avoid this, he is aggressive and bad-tempered. Go near his body and he is covered with needles that are deadly to the touch. Be aware when he speaks, he spits and it will be deadly. He lives in the next cave and he will appear very friendly at first. But be warned, don't be fooled by this."

"What does he look like?" Sophie asked.

Flutterbye replied to Sophie: "In your fantasy books, almost like a dragon, but he breathes no fire."

Luke had always wanted to meet a dragon. Once, he had dreamt about a big orange one. He lived in a cave with two other dragons. They were all friendly towards him. He climbed on one of their necks and flew over his school, waving to all of his friends. The dragon was called Nillbolla from his stories at home. Some dragons were friendly while others were aggressive and angry. This dragon sounded the same but of course, it was real and not just a dream. Sophie had never dreamt of dragons; she had seen them on films. There was silence around them. The bags of teeth made their arms and shoulders very sore and tired, getting heavier all the time. Being humans, Luke and Sophie got hungry. Flutterbye sensed it. In the dragon's cave, pink flowers grew, which humans could eat without any harm to them. They would have to pick them when the dragon was missing. He would not allow anyone to take part of his cave and that included fairies, but to survive, they would have to pick the pink flowers. Flutterbye stopped walking and explained about the flowers to her friends. As soon as they reached the cave, they must start picking them. The more they picked the more meals they would have. As soon as the dragon appeared, if he did, they would have to stop. The pink flowers could be squashed down into the top of the bags containing the teeth. "We are here, my friends," Flutterbye cried, "So, pick as many as you can before the dragon appears."

The cave was much bigger than the previous ones. The dragon needed the space to live and to breathe. They entered the cave which felt very damp. You could see a little light. The first thing that the children noticed was the lovely smell and the walls of the cave covered in pink flowers. They looked like white primroses and the smell was so strong that you could only feel the damp and not smell it. No sign of the dragon. They knew what they must do, so opening all their bags, they started to pick the flowers pushing them down into the top of each bag. The flowers were very easy to pull from the cave walls. One by one, they picked them and one by one was the only way they could be picked. Luke tried to pick three out of the cave wall without any success. They carried on picking, not speaking. All being aware of how quiet this cave was, never stopping until their bags were full, not even to try them to see how they tasted. When they could pick no more, they stopped to try the first pink flower and it tasted really nice. "Be aware, he is coming," Flutterbye whispered so as not to let the dragon hear.

"Are you scared?" Sophie asked Luke. He replied with "Maybe."

"Well, I am," said Sophie.

They finished their third flower as the dragon appeared.

"Why are you stealing my flowers?" the dragon roared.

Flutterbye answered, full of confidence, "The children are hungry, you big clever and handsome dragon."

She was hoping that this would work. The dragon smiled and went all shy and quiet.

"You always tell me how handsome I am, little fairy," he continued, "thank you for your kindness."

Flutterbye looked at the two children, they knew what they must say. Luke was the first.

"I think that you are handsome and so does Sophie."

"Well, say it then," the dragon replied, staring at Sophie with his big brown eyes.

Bravely, Sophie said, "Yes, you are, Mr Dragon. Very handsome and such lovely eyes."

Well, the dragon loved the attention. Looking around his home, he never noticed any of the pink flowers missing. They grew very quickly and the walls were covered once again. Only if they had been caught picking them would he have been angry. Their timing had been just right.

"So, where are you heading?" the dragon asked.

"To save my mother," replied Flutterbye, "Stuttbart and Noose have captured her and taken her below."

"So, you have come to save her," he replied with a smile again.

He seemed very happy for now. Flutterbye knew that it was one of his good days but she also knew that his mood could change very quickly, so they would have to be very careful.

"Take me with you," the dragon said in his next big breath, "I can help you and protect you all."

Flutterbye knew that he could, but at all times, they must keep him happy, which could be very difficult. You could not argue with the dragon, it would make him mad and then they had no chance. *Maybe he would get fed up and then return to his cave,* thought Flutterbye.

"Yes, of course, you can protect us," she said.

Luke and Sophie looked at each other and then back at Flutterbye. *Is she mad?* they thought.

Not knowing why Flutterbye had suggested this, the dragon smiled again and felt excited about his journey. He was bored always doing the same things. There was only so much a dragon could do. He would wake up, guard his cave and then go back to sleep, pretty boring for a dragon. So, it was agreed and all four would be going to meet the Tabots.

"Are you hungry?" the dragon asked with a large grin on his handsome face.

"No, we are stuffed," replied Luke, forgetting that they had stuffed themselves with the dragon's pink flowers.

"Yes," Flutterbye replied as she knew that the dragon was very clever. He knew that there was no food to eat except for his wonderful flowers.

"Try these," he said as he picked about twelve of them. All three of them were really full but so as not to upset the dragon, they each accepted four of the flowers, eating them like they were totally new to them.

It was then that Flutterbye knew just what to say.

"Humans have very tiny stomachs just like us fairies and four pink flowers are quite enough, thank you, Mr Dragon."

He smiled again, so happy that they so liked his flowers which only grew in his cave and no one else's. Luke thought how nice the dragon had been and so did Sophie. Had Flutterbye got it wrong about his bad and dangerous moods? They must remember she knew about them. They must be careful of the dragon even though it was very hard to believe. The dragon liked them too. Especially the little pretty one called Sophie.

"Can we ride on your back, Mr Dragon?" Sophie asked him bravely.

He replied with, "Yes, with pleasure." So, one by one, they climbed onto his back. His dangerous needles were on each side of his body and when in a good mood, you could use them as steps to climb onto the top where there were no spikes at all. How strange it felt to the children to be riding on top of a dragon. Flutterbye was used to this. This was the third time and she always enjoyed it. In fact, it was the safest place to be when he was in such a good mood.

"First, we must take you to the waterfall and change you into a human," the dragon roared.

He knew the journey well, as together, they flew up and up until they reached the waterfall. The dragon came to rest at the entrance and Flutterbye climbed down the needles making sure that the dragon's mood was still the same. As she appeared on the other side, the children saw the little blonde girl with plaits that they remember Flutterbye being before. Shaking off the water left on her arms, she returned to the others and mounted the dragon's back once more. Gone were her two pretty wings and her pretty clothes. Now, she looked the same as the others. As they flew again back down to the depths of the underworld, through all of the levels at a fantastic speed. Luke and Sophie loved it and so too did Flutterbye. It was good to rest her wings again. The heat was again rising quickly. As they flew nearer and nearer towards the Tabots, Stuttbart and Noose were further behind than the others. They felt that there was no rush. The Tabots would be busy working, it was better to contact the commander after they retired for the night. Flueller also tried to slow them down as she had a feeling that the others would follow and how right she was.

"Does the dragon get tired?" Sophie whispered to Flutterbye.

The dragon overheard Sophie and replied with, "Never in a million years do I get tired. We dragons never sleep, we have what we call a few winks but never many."

Yes, thought Flutterbye, *he is still in a good mood. By the time they reached the Tabots' camp, maybe he would be moody and take it out on the Tabots instead of them.* Luke hoped that the trip would never end. It was the best experience of his life and soon, it would be coming to an end.

Chapter Eleven
Dragon Temper

The dragon flight was finally about to be over and still; the dragon was in a very good mood. As much as he had a bad side, his good side was very special and he was very kind. He had really enjoyed bringing the children and the fairy here. *Maybe*, he was thinking, *he could suggest bringing them back*. Flueller, Stuttbart and Noose had made very good timing and they had finally caught the dragon up.

Although the dragon had settled to rest a few times on their journey. The dragon saw them first, approaching.

"Who dares to pass me and my friends?" he shouted.

Stuttbart and Noose were very surprised to see the dragon and a little scared too. They had heard many a story about his temper and his moods. Treading carefully as they passed his huge body, "We are escorting this fairy to meet our commander," Noose shouted to the dragon.

The dragon was quiet for a moment, bowing his head low towards the ground.

"You dare lie to me!" he shouted to Noose who looked very scared by now. The others could all see that the dragon started to get angry, which meant that not just Noose, but all of them, were in danger. Once his mood really started to change, someone must calm him down quickly. All their minds thought alike, but how could they change his mood and soon? Being the queen of the fairies, Flueller had an idea.

"Mr Dragon," she cried, "how would you like some new teeth, super human from many mouths on the surface, magic teeth which will never wear out. Well, what do you think, Mr Dragon?"

Another silence and then he spoke.

"How many teeth?" he asked them.

"How many would make you happy?" Flueller asked him smiling.

"Well, let me see," he replied touching his teeth with one of his large hands.

Opening his mouth, Flueller realised there were a lot of teeth and a lot of gaps too. After carrying the five bags all the way down here for a very good reason, she thought that it had all been a waste of time.

"Hmm," the dragon said, "hmm," once again. "Many many teeth, hundreds in fact."

"Anything to make you happy," Flueller chanted.

"And where do you think you are going?" the dragon roared.

It was too late; his mood was changing and he was very unhappy. His spikes on his sides started to grow. His face started to grow at the same time. Everyone looked very scared as the dragon raised his huge head from the ground. It was time to run. The dragon was ready for the kill and no one would stand in his way, especially silly little ugly creatures called Tabots. Sophie tried to grab hold of Luke's hand before she started to run for her life. Flueller and Flutterbye did the same and the two Tabots grabbed each other and ran too.

Everyone ran in different directions but it did not worry the dragon at all. He hated them all now. They were all his enemies and all of them needed to be killed and he was the one that would be doing it, not the crazy, dirty Tabots or any other silly creatures on the levels he had come across before. No one could outdo his fierce and aggressive energy, just no one.

He appeared to be double the size now. Appearing very large before them, he was very scary and all of them never believed for one moment that they could stay alive. His power was too great as the needles left his body and stabbed Stuttbart to death. Moments later, they reached Noose and death was instant. As he fell to the ground below, aiming for Luke next, he suddenly began to feel calm once again and everything seemed alright with his world. Slowly, the spikes on his back started to disappear and he began to shrink very slowly back to his normal size. His eyes began to lose their evil looks and a large smile appeared on Mr Dragon's face.

"Well, well," he cried, "it's turned out to be a lovely day after all."

The children could not believe the change in the dragon, being scared to move in case he suddenly became miserable and moody once again. Flueller was nowhere to be seen and for one moment, the children had thought that she had been killed. She had been hiding in some bushes so she was safe, unlike the two Tabots guards, who would never have a chance to be famous. Luke, Sophie and Flutterbye stood very still as the dragon continued to talk.

"They were okay, I suppose, but Tabots have a stupid streak in them sometimes, just like me."

He seemed to the others to be apologising about his bad behaviour in a funny sort of way.

"You see," he continued, "most of the time, I am happy but now and again I need to show my temper, are you like that?" he said, looking at Sophie with his huge brown eyes.

Sophie could see that they were full of kindness. So she felt happy to answer the dragon's questions.

"I knew a girl at school, she made me unhappy until Luke sorted her out and she never bullied me again."

"Did she have spikes on her back?" the dragon asked Sophie.

Laughing, Sophie answered the dragon, "No, thank goodness. Although," she said quickly, hoping not to upset the dragon again, "your spikes are very special, Mr Dragon. They have killed two Tabots who were on a mission to take Flueller away from her daughter Flutterbye and that's just not fair."

So, the dragon continued, "Do you think, Sophie, that I have been bad today?"

Remembering never to upset the dragon again, Sophie replied, "Oh, of course, you have not."

All their lives would be in danger, and that was not the answer in reaching the lowest level to return with the fairies' family. Flueller returned from the bush she had been hiding behind and it was time for yet another reunion and more hugs. Flueller knew that Mr Dragon must not feel left out from this so she patted his large head as he bent down to the ground to join in. *This was the best part of the making up,* he thought. *At least humans and fairies were clever at that.*

Chapter Twelve
What Next?

After a few moments, they all sat down around the dragon. Stuttbart and Noose had vanished with the Tabot race. No bodies would ever be found. This was the way of their world.

"With regard to our plans," Flueller asked the others, "do we face more danger or go back to the surface?"

She waited for one of them to reply but no one knew what they wanted to do. The shock of the last event here in the underworld was all too much and Flueller knew it was time to return until another time. A safer time to return and rescue her beloved family. She knew her words and decisions would be enough as she repeated to them all three times.

"We must go back until it is right to return again. We are all very tired and the children need to be with their families again."

"But what about your family?" Sophie asked Flueller.

"For now, I have my daughter back," replied Flueller as both fairies hugged each other.

"So, do we go back?" asked Luke.

"We go back," replied the two fairies together.

So, the journey, for now, was coming to an end. As Flutterbye and Flueller used the last of their fairy dust to take them all back to their home below the mushrooms except, of course, the dragon. He was happy to stay where he was for now.

"Well, my friends," he said as he lowered his back on the ground, "we must part until we meet again."

Luke and Sophie felt very sad to be leaving. They knew that they would all be meeting again, even Mr Dragon, but happy, not angry. It was far safer that way. Flueller shook the fairy dust over them all, except the dragon. They then found themselves back in the safety of the fairies' home, exhausted but happy that they were so safe again. Flueller felt that the sooner the children were back in their own homes, the better. They needed to reunite with their families, although their families never knew about their absence. Luke looked at Sophie and then back at the two little fairies.

"We will come back and help you if you will let us," he said.

Flutterbye replied with, "When you and we are ready, we will know, we must bid you farewell now and we will always remember your courage and determination."

They had a last hug before they left.

Luke said to Flueller, "Remember, we want to help you when you return to the underworld."

"Yes," replied Flueller, "this is a promise."

Suddenly, the children realised they were standing on the green grass around the three mushrooms and all was quiet in the garden. As they walked back to Sophie's house, "Sophie" called Mrs Barker from the house, "Hurry up, you will be late for the party."

They both looked at each other and smiled. Nothing had changed here on this level, nothing.

The End